RIVER OF PERIL

Goldtown Adventures Series

.

GOLDTOWN ADVENTURES #4

RIVER
OF
PERIL

SUSAN K. MARLOW

Kregel
Publications

Printed in the United States of America
15 16 17 18 / 5 4 3 2

Contents

⊰ CHAPTER 1 ⊱

The Secret

CENTRAL VALLEY, CALIFORNIA, 1864

Something's not right.

Jem Coulter could feel it clear to his toes, and he shivered—which was ridiculous. He shouldn't be shivering, not when a hot, late-summer breeze was whipping through the stagecoach. Not when, in less than a day, he'd be in Sacramento, the capital of California. Tall buildings, paddle-wheel boats along the wharf, and more people than Jem had seen in all his twelve years awaited him. He should be tingly with excitement, not shivering in uncertainty.

Jem rested his arms against the window ledge, watched the flat, brown landscape rush by, and tried to push his uneasiness to a little-used corner of his mind.

There was plenty else to occupy his thoughts. The end of September was coming fast, and Jem would soon be trapped in a stuffy schoolroom. His freedom ended, chores and school would take all his time, and summer's heat would give way to rain and mud.

But that didn't make Jem shiver. He was used to school

. . . and to chores . . . and to muddy streets and rain. *If we're lucky, Goldtown might even see snow this winter.* It happened occasionally, transforming the mucky streets and shoddy building fronts into the likeness of a sparkly winter scene from Aunt Rose's calendar.

Jem shivered again and poked his head out the square opening. A cloud of dust from the horses' beating hooves blasted him in the face. He coughed, then squinted and looked up toward the high seat on top of the coach. *Pa's all in a tangle about something,* he told himself. *Something more than just a trip to Sacramento. He won't say, but I can tell he's—*

"Jeremiah Isaiah, get back inside the coach this instant. The very idea!"

Jem jerked around just as one of the wheels hit a hole in the road. *Thud!* Pain shot through his head. He crumpled to his seat and rubbed behind his ears, wishing he were anyplace but inside this rocking rattletrap. Panning for gold in the last, muddy dribbles of Cripple Creek was better than being churned like butter for two days.

"Why can't I ride up with Pa and Walt?" he burst out. The back of his head throbbed. "It's so hot in here I'm frying. At least up top, I—" Jem broke off in sudden realization that he'd overstepped his bounds. But it was too late to take back his words.

Aunt Rose pressed her lips together, and her face scrunched up in a familiar *mind-your-tongue* expression. He'd seen the look often enough during the five months his aunt and his cousin, Nathan, had lived with the Coulter family. He also knew he'd have received more than Auntie's look if three other passengers had not been along for the ride.

Sitting stiff and formal on the seat across from him, Mr. Watson, Mrs. Graham, and Mrs. Fields were also giving Jem "the look." He knew just what they were thinking: *Jeremiah*

Coulter, sheriff's son, you had better be a proper example every waking minute of every livelong day.

One of the hardships of having a sheriff for a father.

He saw Ellie and Nathan hunch back into their seats, trying to avoid the trouble. All four grown-ups in the cramped coach seemed to be circling Jem like hungry hawks, waiting for him to speak. And it had better be the right words, *or else.*

Jem reddened, straightened his shoulders, and swallowed. "I'm sorry, Aunt Rose, for the way I spoke to you." He really *was* sorry, but he hated having to tell her so in front of these other prune-faced busybodies.

With proper conduct restored, the grown-ups went back to chatting about topics of no interest to Jem. He went back to staring out the window—and saw the dried-up stream bed only seconds before the stage plunged over it.

The coach lurched violently forward, then with a sharp jerk pitched backward. Wheels bounced over rocks and ruts. Most of the passengers were lifted out of their seats and fell into each others' laps.

Jem gripped the window rim with all his might. He'd had plenty of practice holding on during the past two days. He had no desire to fly into Mr. Watson, his skinny Sunday school teacher, or break the man's spectacles.

His ten-year-old sister didn't fare so well. Plump Mrs. Graham groaned when Ellie fell headlong into her lap. One of Ellie's auburn braids slapped the woman across the mouth. Mrs. Graham gasped and flung her fleshy arms over her head.

A few seconds later, the stage was over the creek bed and back on smoother ground. Jem grabbed Ellie and plopped her down safely beside him.

"At least she's nice and squishy," Ellie whispered when everyone's arms and legs had been sorted out.

"It's better that *you* landed in *her* lap than if *she* had landed on *you*," Jem replied softly in Ellie's ear. *Very* softly. He kept his face stone sober.

Ellie's high-pitched giggles filled the stagecoach. They echoed above the rattling coach and over the women's voices. Mrs. Fields frowned, and Ellie choked back her laughter before Aunt Rose could silence her.

The road stayed mostly level after that. The rocking and swaying of the stagecoach began to lull Jem into a quiet-but-queasy state. He yawned, but he didn't relax completely. Any minute an unexpected hole might reach out and grab the coach. It was best to stay alert, no matter how sleepy he felt.

He glanced down. Ellie had fallen asleep in the afternoon heat. Her tousled head lay limply in his aunt's lap. Aunt Rose sat straight-backed, her hands draped across Ellie to keep her from slipping. Sitting on her far side, Cousin Nathan stared listlessly out the window. It was clear that traveling by stagecoach was neither one's fondest activity.

Now Jem knew why. He'd traveled by stage more than once in his life. It had always been an exciting adventure, mostly because the driver let Jem sit up top. *Not* stuffed in a coach for hours and days on end. Jem's stage trips had also been short—no more than an hour or so.

But two days? Twenty hours in a stagecoach was about eighteen hours too long in Jem's mind. Nathan and Aunt Rose had traveled by stage at least that long when they'd come to Goldtown last spring. No wonder they looked like they wanted off. *I want off too.*

Jem shivered again—the same eerie shiver that had pestered him ever since Pa had announced they were going to Sacramento for a week. Jem had never been farther than Mariposa in his life, so the news should have sent him running to pack. Ellie had certainly celebrated. Nathan too. Even Aunt Rose clasped her hands together and exclaimed, "Oh, Matthew, it's been so long since I've been to the city!"

But something in his father's eyes kept Jem from jumping for joy. His worry grew when Pa insisted that Jem ride in the coach with the others, even though there was plenty of room with the driver.

"Why, Pa?" he asked. "I always ride up top."

"Just do it, Son. Bring along a book—maybe that new dime novel I saw you slip under your shirt after services last Sunday." Pa had grinned and ruffled Jem's hair, but Jem didn't smile back.

Now he looked around the coach and muttered, "Pa expects me to *read*? When I'm rattling around worse than gravel in Strike's rocker?"

The thought of the Coulter family's prospector-friend, Strike-it-rich Sam, made Jem feel around in his trouser pocket for his ever-present gold pouch. Last spring, standing knee-deep in icy, snow-melted Cripple Creek, Jem had heard Strike boast that 1864 would be a good gold-panning year. Jem didn't agree at the time. His pan came up empty more times than it showed color.

But in the end, the old miner had been right.

Jem fingered his pouch. *I haven't done too badly this year.* He'd managed to coax more flakes, dust, and pea-sized nuggets out of the creek than he had in past years. Best of all, Jem had panned a thumb-sized chunk just a few weeks ago. Mr. Watson—the assayer sitting across from him—assured Jem it was indeed an ounce.

A whole ounce! Sixteen dollars' worth. A fortune to Jem. He kept his prize hidden away in his attic bedroom. Every few days he took the nugget out, just to admire it and imagine all the things he could buy with that one little hunk of gold.

"And what can I buy in the city with *this*?" Jem whispered to himself, squeezing his pouch. A few months ago, he'd have spent it all to help Pa run their broken-down ranch. But now, with Pa accepting the sheriff job and Aunt Rose running the house, it wasn't as hard to make ends meet. "It's not enough for a rifle, but I betcha I can buy a new knife."

Jem carefully withdrew his hand from his pocket. Not even Ellie or Nathan knew he'd brought along his gold stash—though Ellie could probably guess. She was always quick to figure out what he was thinking.

Careful to keep his head inside the coach, Jem peered through the window and wondered again what his father was up to. Some kind of secret sheriff business, Jem decided. It couldn't be a prisoner transfer, though, unless the desperado was tied to the luggage rack on top or stuffed in the rear boot.

Why, then, was Pa riding shotgun up with Walt? *What are we carrying? And if it's something dangerous, why would Pa bring us along?*

Another shiver.

Aunt Rose reached over Ellie and gave Jem a sharp poke. "Are you catching a chill, Jeremiah? Land sakes, just what we need is for you to come down with a fever. Tell me. Are you feeling poorly?"

"No, ma'am," Jem answered without turning around. His gaze stayed fixed on the wide, flat land, so different from the pine-and-oak-covered foothills around Goldtown. Trees and brush grew here aplenty, but Jem missed the mountains. He shaded his eyes and caught a glimpse of a dark smudge in the distance—the Sierra Nevada.

"Three-thirty," Mr. Watson announced some time later. "Another two hours, and we should arrive in the city." He snapped his pocket watch shut and stuffed it in his vest pocket. Then he drew a handkerchief across his sweat-dotted forehead. "I forgot how hot it gets in this valley. It must be close to a hundred in the shade."

Jem wondered who the assayer was talking to. Auntie's eyes were closed. Nathan was leaning back against the seat with his mouth open, snoring. As usual, a hank of his white-blond hair hung over his eyes. The two other women appeared to be asleep as well.

It finally dawned on Jem that Mr. Watson was directing his remarks at *him*. "Are you sure your watch didn't stop?" Jem answered. "It feels like we've been traveling hours longer than that."

The assayer drew himself up and reached inside his pocket. "I wound that watch only last—"

Crack!

The sound of a gunshot cut through Mr. Watson's words. Two more shots and the *twang* of a bullet across metal brought the coach to a sudden, lurching halt. Horses whinnied, harnesses jingled, and the women shrieked. From outside, Jem heard angry voices.

Ellie woke up with a yelp and clutched Jem's arm. "What happened? Where's Pa?"

Jem tightened his fingers on the window ledge, but he didn't stick his head out to see what was going on. He already knew.

Somebody was holding up the stage.

⊰ CHAPTER 2 ⊱

Holdup

Jem strained his ears to hear what was happening outside. He knew better than to burst through the coach door, even though every part of him itched to rush to Pa's aid. The sound of gunfire kept Jem glued to his seat better than any words from Aunt Rose.

Not that his aunt was saying much. She had her arms wrapped tightly around Ellie and was rocking back and forth. Her lips moved, clearly pleading with the Almighty, but no sound came out.

Jem couldn't have heard her even if she'd been shouting her prayer. He couldn't hear anything over the racket coming from inside the coach. Mrs. Graham and Mrs. Fields shrieked and waved their arms, demanding answers at the top of their lungs. Their pocketbooks and hankies went flying. They cackled worse than a flock of hens cornered by a coyote.

They look like hens too, Jem thought in disgust, *flapping their wings and losing feathers everywhere. Hush!* he wanted to holler.

Mr. Watson's face was pale but set in a look of resolve to see this through. He did his best to soothe the ladies, but Jem could see it wasn't working.

Holdup

Jem scooted closer to the window and carefully pushed his head out a few inches. There was nothing to see. Only horses, brush and trees along the roadside, and in the distance an old wagon.

"Ladies, *please!*"

Jem whipped around at the loud, commanding voice. A man with a head full of curly black hair and a bandana covering half his face stood at the window near Nathan. He raised a Colt .44 pistol and pointed it through the opening. Nathan fell back against the seat with a gasp.

"I really must insist that you be quiet," the highwayman said in a polite-but-firm voice. "They can no doubt hear you all the way back in Jackson. Calm yourselves."

The women fell into shocked silence, and Jem let out a breath of relief. A raised pistol had accomplished what all of Mr. Watson's calm assurances could not—peace and quiet.

"My companions and I have no intention of bringing bodily harm to any of you fine folks," the bandit said. "I only ask that you step out of the coach and stay within sight. We will take what we came for and be on our way as quickly as possible. Then you are free to continue your journey to Sacramento." His eyes smiled, but his gun never wavered.

When no one moved, his eyes turned cold and he yanked open the door. "Get out!"

The reality of being robbed suddenly slammed into Jem. He'd heard plenty of tales of highwaymen robbing stages up and down gold country. But Goldtown lay so far south of the main routes and the richer mines—like Grass Valley and Nevada City—that nobody paid much attention to their little town.

Until today.

What do we have that they want? Jem wondered. Then his hand went to his pocket. They might steal his gold! He gritted his teeth. *Not if I can help it.*

15

Jem hung back while the semi-polite stagecoach robber offered his hand to the women. Quickly, he pulled the pouch from his pocket, opened it, and sprinkled his precious gold inside his right boot. Stamping down hard, the pebbles, dust, and flakes settled around his ankle and under his foot. The nuggets bit into Jem's sole. He winced.

Hurry, hurry! There was no time to worry about comfort. Ellie and Aunt Rose were stepping down from the coach. Only he and Mr. Watson remained. Jem crumpled his empty pouch and stuffed it along the inside of his left boot. Then he slid his trouser legs back in place. Looking up, he caught Mr. Watson giving him a nod of approval.

Jem grinned and hurried out behind Aunt Rose. Instead of jumping off the edge of the coach, he used the narrow, iron rung that passed as a step to carefully lower himself to the ground. Then he straightened up and looked around.

Besides the man who had ordered them out of the coach, three other bandana-masked highwaymen stood around with pistols. They shouted orders at each other and to Pa and the driver sitting up on top. Now that the women had closed their mouths, Jem could clearly hear what the men were saying.

"I won't ask you again, Sheriff," said a tall man dressed in shiny black, knee-high boots and a brown overcoat. "Get down from there or somebody is going to get hurt." He waved his pistol at the seven passengers huddled together a few yards away and sighed. "And we don't want that. We only want the gold."

Jem gasped. *Gold? What gold?* The Midas mine shipped gold and the miners' payroll back and forth, but since when did Mr. Sterling, the mine owner, announce which stage was carrying it?

"You shot the driver," Pa said. "I can't leave him up here to bake in the sun. I need help lowering him to the ground."

He looked angry and frustrated. And helpless. His Henry rifle and his sidearm lay in the dust next to the wheel.

The curly-haired robber nudged Mr. Watson. "Help the sheriff." Then he called up to Pa, "We surely didn't mean no harm to the driver, Sheriff. Just wanted him to stop the stage, but he didn't seem willing. Can I help it if he got in the way of a stray bullet?"

Jem couldn't see the man's mouth, but he heard a chuckle and knew the bandit was grinning behind his makeshift mask. He gave Mr. Watson a poke with his gun to hurry him along. "Get moving. We haven't got all day."

With Mr. Watson's help, Pa lowered the injured driver to the ground and laid him carefully in the shade of the coach, out of the worst of the sun's rays. "Walt," Pa urged, slapping the man's cheeks with a gentle hand. "Wake up. You're winged. It's just a graze. Let's not sleep on the job, my friend."

Pa didn't look or sound too worried over the driver's injury. It appeared he'd already tied up Walt's arm with a bandana to stop the bleeding, and that was that. Why then was Walt unconscious? Was it from fear? Heatstroke? Jem could believe either explanation. His heart thudded from looking at all the guns, and the sun was scorching him and everyone else.

Pa glanced up from Walt and looked over at the passengers. "Is everyone all right?"

Ellie burst into tears. Before Jem or Aunt Rose could stop her, she broke away from the group and ran to Pa. Halfway there, Black Boots caught her arm and yanked her around. "Get back with the others, missy."

Pa jumped to his feet. "Let her go," he ordered in a low voice. "Rob us, cut the horses loose if you must, but leave her be."

"Pa!" Ellie squealed. She landed a vicious kick to her captor's leg, then twisted free. Before anyone could blink, she slammed into Pa. He caught her up in his arms and hugged her tight.

Jem covered his mouth to keep his laughter inside. *Good for you, Ellie!*

But Pa wasn't smiling. Neither was Black Boots. He rubbed his shin and pierced Pa with a steely-gray look. "That kid's slipperier than a greased pig," he muttered, keeping his pistol steady. "Get over there with the others and stay put."

"Whatever you say," Pa said.

Black Boots—clearly the bandits' leader—motioned to his comrades. "Hurry up. Get the strongbox. But have a care," he warned. "It'll be heavier than it looks, on account of this special shipment."

Special shipment? Jem glanced up. "Pa?" he whispered. "What's going on? What kind of special gold are we carrying?"

Pa shook his head, and Jem took the hint. *Be quiet.*

It took three men to jostle the strongbox from under the driver's seat and shove it over the edge. The metal box landed on the ground with a dull, heavy *thud.* A few minutes later, one of the highwaymen brought a wagon around and pulled up next to the stagecoach.

Black Boots held his pistol on the coach passengers while the other three lugged the heavy load up and into the wagon. By the time they finished, they were breathing hard. Sweat poured down their foreheads, soaking their bandanas.

Jem knew why. Pa had shown him a gold bar once when he was Ellie's age. It wasn't very big—about the size of a narrow brick. When Pa grinned and told him to lift it, Jem couldn't. No wonder! Pa said that little gold brick weighed nearly twenty-eight pounds.

The strongbox most likely held eight or ten bars. Jem's heart skipped in astonishment. *Roasted rattlesnakes, that's a lot of gold!* And it was piled into a box no bigger than the small wooden chest that sat at the end of Jem's bed. Where did all that gold come from? Surely not from the Midas mine, which had never been a rich producer.

"No sudden moves, Sheriff," Black Boots said, breaking into Jem's thoughts. He kept his pistol steady and pointed it at Pa, who was still holding Ellie. "We'll be out of your hair in no time."

The curly-haired bandit, recovered from hauling the gold, brought his leader a small pad of paper and a stubby pencil. "Here you go."

Black Boots holstered his gun and took the paper. Frowning, he scribbled rapidly then ripped the paper from the pad and strolled over to Pa. For the first time, he looked apologetic. "Sheriff, I want you to give this letter to the Wells Fargo agent when you arrive in Sacramento." He held it out.

Pa lowered Ellie to the ground and took the paper. He glanced over the words then gave the man a startled look. "What in blazes is the meaning of *this*?" His dark-blue eyes flashed in anger. "Of all the outlandish, deceitful schemes I ever—" He broke off when Black Boots drew his pistol.

"Please, Sheriff," he said. "It is no scheme. We are utterly sincere. The letter you hold is a receipt for funds we are raising for the Confederate army. My associates and I are not bandits—"

"In a pig's eye," Mr. Watson muttered, fists clenched.

Black Boots ignored him. "We belong to the Knights of the Golden Circle, a group of Southern sympathizers. We have just carried out a legitimate military operation in the Union state of California. It is no different from any other wartime engagement, were we on a battleground back in the Atlantic states."

Jem's mouth fell open. To him, the War Between the

States was nothing more than a subject Miss Cheney mentioned when a weeks-old newspaper found its way into their classroom. "History is being made right now," she often said. "Future schoolchildren will one day read about this war. You pupils are *living* it."

Jem knew his cousin had lived the war. Nathan's father had been killed in the Battle of Gettysburg over a year ago. But California—and especially Goldtown—was so far removed from the action that it seemed like just another book lesson to Jem.

He swallowed. Not any longer.

Pa's sharp laugh made Jem jump. "That's absurd. None of this gold will ever see the South."

"I beg to differ with you," Black Boots said. He tapped the letter in Pa's hand. "Keep that receipt safe, Sheriff. When the war is over and the Confederacy emerges victorious, its debts will be graciously repaid."

Pa snorted his disbelief and stuffed the letter into his vest pocket. "I highly doubt that."

"To show our sincerity," the bandit continued as if Pa had not spoken, "we're leaving. We have no intention of robbing civilians. Truly, all we want is the gold." He bowed slightly. "We are, after all, Southern gentlemen."

The three women, who had been clutching their handbags close to their chests, sagged in relief. Jem wiggled his toes and looked forward to returning the hidden gold to his pouch.

The road agent saluted Pa with the tip of his pistol barrel, winked at Ellie, and climbed aboard the wagon's tailgate. "Let's go!" he called to the others. He kept his gun trained on the stage passengers.

The wagon—and Goldtown's gold—rolled away, leaving behind a thick cloud of dust . . . and a disbelieving group of travelers staring after it.

⊰ CHAPTER 3 ⊱

Where's the Gold?

The dust hadn't yet settled when Pa and Mr. Watson rushed over to look after the stage driver. Walt waved away their help and scooted himself up against the coach's wheel. "Hang it all," he said, "I missed the excitement. Did they . . . did they take the box?"

Pa nodded. "I'm afraid so, Walt."

Walt shook his head and let out a disgusted snort. "Don't let the Express office know I keeled over, Matt, or I'll find myself out of a job." He looked down at his shirt sleeve. "Been shot at plenty o' times in my life. Don't know what happened."

"It doesn't matter," Pa said kindly. "What's important is that you're still with us and—"

"*Uncle Matt!*" Nathan's terror-filled shriek brought everyone around. "It's Mother. You have to stop her. Look!" He pointed.

Aunt Rose was dashing down the road, swinging her handbag madly over her head. Her hat had come loose and flown off her head. It lay in the dirt a few steps behind her flying figure. "Come back here, you thieves!" she shouted.

"What in the world!" Pa leaped up and took off after his sister, leaving Jem and the others gaping.

21

"What's the matter with her?" Jem asked his cousin in a hushed voice. Never had he seen his aunt act wildly or out of control. She wasn't one to show her feelings very often. When she did, it was with a quick hug or a few tears—never an outrageous, stomping display like this.

"I dunno," Nathan admitted. "She cried a lot when Father died, but she didn't run crazy with grief through the streets. Maybe . . . maybe the sun got to her."

"She sure looks funny," Ellie said, giggling.

"Ellie!" Jem warned. But he couldn't help agreeing. He clamped his jaw shut to keep from laughing. Did Aunt Rose really think she could overtake the robbers, much less convince them to return their precious load? Not likely!

Jem watched Pa catch up to Aunt Rose, put an arm across her shoulders, and hug her. Then he turned her around, and together they headed back. Pa stopped once. He scooped Auntie's hat off the ground and plopped it on her head. Dust puffed around her like a halo, and Pa gave her another hug.

Both were laughing by the time they reached the others.

"I declare, Matthew! I don't know what came over me," Aunt Rose was saying. Tears rolled down her cheeks. "I suppose the injustice of it all—the very *gall* of those Rebels—exploded from me like a cannon shot. Dear Frederick in his grave, and now they dare to steal our gold! I couldn't stop myself from going after them." She wiped her eyes and dissolved into another round of laugher. "Dear me, I must have looked a sight."

"Like a lunatic," Pa admitted, chuckling. "Scared Nathan half to death."

Aunt Rose laid a gentle hand against Nathan's cheek. "I *am* sorry, Son." Her eyes twinkled—just like Pa's did when he told a funny story.

Nathan laughed, clearly relieved that his mother wasn't crazy after all, and Jem joined in. Soon, the rest of the passengers—even injured Walt—were snickering. The worry of the last half hour melted away.

"It's a real shame you didn't go after them with a pistol, Rose," Mrs. Fields said, clucking her tongue. "You could have shot at those *fine*, Southern gentlemen on our behalf."

"I don't think it would have ended well if she had," Pa said, frowning slightly. He helped Aunt Rose into the stage and motioned the rest of the passengers to climb aboard. "We've had a good laugh, folks, but I'm afraid we won't be laughing for long. As soon as those 'Knights' shoot off the lock and discover what they really took, they'll be after us like a prairie fire. It's time to go."

Walt caught his breath. "You mean . . . ?"

Pa nodded. "The gold's inside, concealed under the seats. You've all been sitting on top of eighty-five thousand dollars' worth of gold bullion bound for the Union."

Gasps greeted Pa's announcement.

"Saints preserve us!" Mrs. Graham whispered. She clutched her throat and fell heavily into her seat. "How did those bandits know we—"

"Goldtown has its share of Southern supporters, Mrs. Graham," Pa broke in. "Somebody must have leaked the news. Nobody was supposed to know." He smiled at the injured driver. "Sorry, Walt, not even you."

Jem wanted to crow his delight. *I knew something wasn't quite right.* His shivers and uneasiness *had* meant something. Pa had been hiding a dangerous secret. Now that it was out in the open, Jem could relax and enjoy the rest of the trip.

A few awkward moments passed while Pa and Walt argued about who should drive the rest of the way. Pa won, and the stage driver was hustled aboard. Jem groaned. The coach was cramped enough without an extra—

"Jem," Pa said from the driver's seat, "you might as well give Walt your spot in the coach and ride up with me. The worst has happened—we've been robbed. But if we move right along, we're probably safe enough. Sacramento is less than two hours away."

Jem leaped to obey before Pa changed his mind. He clambered over the front wheel and up to the high seat. He heard Ellie beg to ride up top, and Nathan chimed in, "It's not fair!"

Jem looked around. Sometimes, a passenger carved out an extra spot for himself next to a satchel or a small trunk, but not on this trip. Luggage was crammed into every square inch on the stagecoach's roof. The driver's seat, however, looked roomy enough to squeeze a couple of extra kids aboard.

Pa shook his head at the children's pleading and said they'd have to take turns. Then he asked Mr. Watson to join him up top. "So long as you're not afraid to handle a rifle," he added.

"I can shoot—like everybody else in Goldtown," the assayer assured Pa. He settled himself in the high seat next to Jem and took the Henry rifle. "I just don't guarantee I'll hit anything."

Pa chuckled. "Hope you don't have to." He released the brake, slapped the reins over the horses' backs, and they were off on the final stretch of road.

The trip had improved considerably for Jem, except for one small detail. He yanked off his left boot, fished around for his empty gold pouch, and wedged the boot beside him. Then he began to remove his right boot.

"What are you doing?" Pa asked, sparing a quick glance at his son. He jiggled the reins to keep the horses hurrying along.

"I—" A small rut made the coach lurch to one side. Jem slammed into Pa. The ride up here was no smoother than down below. "I stashed my gold in my boots so the bandits couldn't"—another jounce—"steal it. But the nuggets are giving me blisters."

It would take a steady hand, which was nearly impossible on this ride, to return the gold to Jem's pouch. After a couple of awkward attempts, Mr. Watson offered to pour the contents of Jem's boot back in place. Goldtown's assayer had the steadiest hands in town, and Jem didn't lose even a flake.

"Thanks, Mr. Watson." Jem tightened the leather cord and stuffed his precious bundle back in his pocket. "There. Safe and sound."

"You didn't tell me you were bringing your life's savings to the city," Pa remarked.

"All but my big nugget," Jem said, grinning. "And you didn't tell *me* you were guarding thousands of dollars in gold. Is that why we came along? To make it look like it was just another ordinary, everyday stage run?"

"In part." Then, "Hold on!"

The stage blundered over an exceptionally rough spot for a full minute. Jem gripped the back of the seat and pressed his feet against the footboard to steady himself. A grim-faced Mr. Watson clutched the rifle and tried to keep his place.

"What a lousy road," Pa griped when the stagecoach quit bouncing. He shook his head. "I told Ernest Sterling it would be better to take the gold straight to Stockton. It's closer, and the road's gotta be better than this. Stockton has a deepwater port. One stop, and his precious Union gold would be aboard a seagoing vessel."

Jem didn't know if Pa was talking to him or to Mr. Watson. *Probably neither one of us. He's just complaining out loud.*

"You know Sterling," Mr. Watson said. "He's as hardheaded as the ore in his mine. He's always dealt with his own people in Sacramento—some cousin or another—and he likes to do things his way." He glanced over Jem's head at Pa. "So, this is the gold he promised the Union?"

"Yep." Pa nodded. "I think by now the whole town knows the Midas finally hit a bonanza in those newly opened tunnels."

I didn't know! Jem thought. But then, he rarely visited town except to deliver firewood. No time to loiter on the streets and listen to gossip when he had work to do. He scowled. Apparently, none of his chums at Sunday school had thought to let him in on Goldtown's biggest news since the stamp mill reopened. *Why didn't Pa tell me?*

He opened his mouth to ask, but then quickly clamped it shut. He always learned more when he kept quiet and let the grown-ups talk.

"Finally," Pa was saying, "a chance for Goldtown to do its share for the war effort. You can't keep something like this quiet for long. No sirree, not when folks read that General Grant himself says he didn't know what he'd do without California gold."

Mr. Watson nodded. "Yes, I'd say eighty-five thousand dollars' worth of gold is quite a bonanza. And it assayed out as high-grade ore. But I had no idea how Sterling planned to transport such a rich shipment back East."

"No one was supposed to know," Pa said. "Ship the gold by stage to Sacramento, then downriver to San Francisco by steamboat. Sterling kept everybody guessing when he hired extra guns on every stage the past few weeks. A diversion of sorts."

Mr. Watson grunted. "That obviously didn't work."

That's for sure! Jem agreed silently.

"Sterling decided it was a good sign when none of the other stages were held up," Pa said with a shrug. "He tried to make it even less obvious by asking me to bring my family along on this trip." Pa reached out and squeezed Jem's shoulder.

Jem looked up. "Does Aunt Rose know the real reason you took us along?"

Pa shook his head. "She doesn't even suspect, being caught up in the excitement of visiting the city." He leaned over and whispered in Jem's ear, "Mr. Sterling is paying our expenses. Just so long as I make sure the gold ends up on the right boat."

Now that Pa had turned his attention away from Mr. Watson, Jem felt free to ask one of the questions swirling around in his head. "What's in the strongbox the bandits took?"

Pa threw his head back and laughed, which startled Mr. Watson and made Jem grin. "If it wasn't so serious, I'd laugh all the way to the city," he said. "It's lead. A *lot* of lead. But lead's not near as heavy as gold, so we had to pack the strongbox clear to the top to make it feel genuine."

"But . . ." Jem's voice trailed off.

"But what, Son?"

"What if they'd opened the box right away to make sure it was the real thing?"

Pa jiggled the reins, urging the horses forward a little faster. "I worried about that," he admitted. "In that case, they would have taken the gold."

"You'd have told them where it was?"

"Of course," Pa said. "No gold—not even for the sake of the Union—is worth putting my family and the other passengers in danger." Then he smiled. "But the strongbox was heavy, and they were obviously in a hurry. So, our scheme worked . . . for now. I only hope their hideout is far enough away to give us time to reach the *New World*. I'll breathe easier when the Midas gold is safely aboard the steamer to San Francisco."

Jem was already breathing easier. He now looked forward to seeing Sacramento, especially since Mr. Sterling was paying for it. He doubted Aunt Rose knew *that*. Learning the rich mine owner was paying their expenses would have made anybody—even his aunt—suspicious enough to ask why.

When Pa slowed down and told Jem to swap places with Nathan, he didn't protest. A few minutes later, in spite of the swaying coach, Jem let himself relax and doze off. The excitement he'd shoved to the back of his mind now spilled over into his dreams. The State Fair, horse racing, seeing a steamboat, spending his gold—everything weaved in and out of his drowsy mind.

He jerked awake when Pa pulled the stagecoach to a rough stop. Rubbing his gritty eyes, Jem peeked out the window and took his first look at the capital of California. He couldn't see much. The Wells Fargo Express office took up his entire view. It looked just like the Express office in Goldtown, only this building was two stories high. And the paint was fresher. Plus, it sported a wide awning that reached out and shaded the sidewalk. Fancy, indeed.

Jem wasn't sure what he'd hear on his very first visit to the big city. A steamboat's whistle? The rattling of traffic along brick streets? Music spilling from an opera house?

What he didn't expect to hear was his father's voice drowning out all other sounds. "What do you mean, the *New World* hasn't docked yet?"

Jem's heart skipped a beat. If the side-wheeler wasn't at the wharf, then what would Pa do with all that gold?

⊰ CHAPTER 4 ⊱

Welcome to the City

Without waiting for Aunt Rose's permission, Jem unlatched the door and hopped down from the stagecoach to find out what was happening. Quick as a spider, Ellie scurried after him. Jem shot a glance at Pa and the Express agent. Surely his father wouldn't mind if his children wanted to stretch their legs and walk around on solid ground after two days of being jostled.

Pa didn't tell Jem to get back inside the coach. He paid no attention to his children at all. Arms crossed and clearly unhappy at the unexpected news, he stood listening to an older man.

Jem hurried to get out of the street. Instead of dust, his boots slapped against hard cobblestone. *No muddy streets in the winter,* he thought. It wasn't a noble first impression of the capital, but it was practical. Mud got mighty tiresome. He grinned at the solid brick under his feet. *I like Sacramento already!*

"When will the steamer dock?" Pa was asking when Jem and Ellie came up beside him. He spared them a brief look then turned back to the agent.

The man shrugged. "Dunno. Tomorrow? The next day?

When it comes to a side-wheeler, who can tell? She might be waiting for the tide down at the delta. Maybe her boiler's acting up. Then again, maybe she's churning upriver extra slow on account of—"

"All right," Pa interrupted with a heavy sigh. "I'm sorry for snapping at you. It's been a long two days, and I have important cargo for the *New World*."

The Wells Fargo agent was an aging man who seemed to move at half the speed of everyone else on the busy sidewalk. He scratched his whiskers and said, "You young'uns are sure in a hurry nowadays. And everyone insists their cargo is important. If you're all that fired up, you should head down to the river and ask the harbormaster." He waved a careless hand to his right. "If anybody knows about delays, it's Steve."

Pa nodded. "I'll do that, just as soon as I make arrangements for this shipment. I'm Ernest Sterling's agent from Goldtown. We're expected."

A light came on in the old man's eyes. "Ah, yes!" He chuckled. "I understand your hurry. You'll want to speak to Mr. Fitzgerald." He crooked a finger. "Come along with me, sonny. He's inside, working on the books."

For a horrible second, Jem thought the Express agent was speaking to *him*. When Pa obediently stepped behind the man, Jem realized he was addressing Pa. Jem had never heard anybody call Pa "sonny" before, not even Strike-it-rich Sam.

Jem settled himself against the hitching rail and watched the two men disappear into the office. The door clicked shut behind them, a clear warning that Pa wanted to discuss matters in private.

Jem took the hint and made himself comfortable. It might be a long time before his father emerged from the Express office. After all, he had to make arrangements to keep eighty-five thousand dollars' worth of gold safe. No easy

task. There was always a chance the Knights of the Golden Circle had discovered Pa's trick and were even now lurking in the streets of Sacramento, spying on them.

Jem grew alert at the thought and suddenly realized how unguarded the stagecoach looked. Then again, Pa probably figured it was better to keep the everyday-stage-trip deception going until the gold was stashed someplace safe. An armed guard standing around would let more than the Knights know that something of extra value was on board.

A murmur of ladies' voices and the rustling of skirts told Jem that the other passengers had stepped down. They stood around, waiting for something. It took Jem a minute to figure out they were waiting for their baggage.

"Where's Walt?" he asked, looking around for the injured driver.

Aunt Rose shoved a dirty strand of hair under her hat and pinned it back in place. "I believe Mr. Watson hurried him off to see a doctor. The poor man was looking mighty puny by the time we pulled in."

Mrs. Graham wagged her head. Her double chin quivered. "I understand the need for medical care, but land sakes! Wells Fargo could at least send someone out to unload our bags." She turned a scowling face toward the building. "What a muddle this trip has turned into."

Aunt Rose drew herself up and faced the older woman. "We can thank the good Lord and my brother that our trip ended safely, Lois. And seeing to the safety of our special cargo is surely worth a few minutes' delay."

"I meant no disrespect, Rose," Mrs. Graham apologized quickly. "But I would like my luggage before sundown."

As if in answer to her complaint, the door opened and a wiry young man hurried out. He muttered an apology for the delay then climbed to the top of the coach and began untying the baggage. One by one, carpetbags, small trunks, and satchels dropped to the ground. In Goldtown, the bags would have instantly been shrouded in a thick cloud of dust; here they only made loud *plopping* noises as they hit the brick street.

By the time the baggage was piled up on the sidewalk, Pa and four Express agents had made their appearance. Two other men accompanied them, rifles and sidearms in full view. Pa reached up onto the high driver's seat, grabbed his rifle, and nodded.

Without being told, the Goldtown passengers moved off. Jem grabbed Ellie's hand and yanked her out of the way. Nathan ducked behind Jem.

"I wanna see!" Ellie told Jem, ripping her hand from his. She took a step forward, but Jem held her back.

"It's just a couple of strongboxes," he told her.

Jem's eyes grew wide as he watched how fast the men worked. He didn't know how they did it, but someone opened the space under the seats and hauled out the gold before Jem could count to twenty. By the time he reached fifty, both of the heavy boxes had vanished inside the Express office.

Pa joined his family on the sidewalk five minutes later. He was smiling, and the worry lines on his forehead had smoothed out. He let out a long, tired breath. "Well, that's that. For now, anyway."

"Where's the gold, Pa?" Ellie asked. Her hazel eyes sparkled with interest.

Pa tweaked one of her braids. "Tucked away in the Wells Fargo safe. Signed for and out of my hair for a day or two." He wiped a shirt sleeve across his forehead. "I confess my stomach's been churning ever since I agreed to see the Midas gold safely shipped out. It's secure for now, but I won't sleep well until I see the *New World* chugging downriver with the gold on board."

He chuckled. "It will then be someone else's problem." He wiped his hands together, as if he'd just brushed away a distasteful job. "I have to go down to the wharf and talk to the harbormaster. Would anybody like to tag along, or are you all too worn out from the trip?"

Jem let out a whoop of delight. The hours of weary traveling fell from his shoulders and he felt wide awake. "I'm not tired. I'd like to go."

"Me too!" Ellie and Nathan chorused.

Aunt Rose glanced around at the deepening twilight. "It will be sundown before long, Matthew. Shouldn't we settle into our accommodations first?" She clasped her handbag and let out a weary sigh. "And there is the matter of supper to consider."

The word "supper" set Jem's stomach growling. He hadn't eaten since well before noon. The stage had pulled into a tiny way station for a ten-minute stop while the horses were changed. Three bites of stew, a hunk of coarse bread, and they were on their way again.

Jem patted his empty belly. "Supper sounds good."

"The hotel is just down the block from here," Pa said. "But we'll have to hurry. It's getting late, and I can't afford to put off finding out when we can expect the *New World*." He turned to Jem. "Stay with your aunt while I find somebody to help with our luggage. I'll be right back."

Jem nodded. He noticed that the Coulter family stood alone next to a shrinking pile of baggage. The other stage passengers had left to complete whatever business or pleasure had brought them to Sacramento. Even the stagecoach had vanished, to be cleaned and readied for another trip.

Ten minutes later, Jem stepped over the threshold of the Union Hotel . . . and froze. Craning his neck until he was sure it would snap off, he gawked at the enormous, ornate light fixture dangling overhead from the lobby's ceiling. Dozens of tiny gas lamps and crystal prisms made the whole thing dance with a thousand sparkly lights.

"It's like a million diamonds," Ellie said in a hushed voice.

Jem didn't answer. Instead, he pulled his gaze from the spectacle and followed Pa toward the counter. Nearby, men and women slicked up in fancy clothes strolled to and fro through the hotel. Young men wearing snappy hotel attire followed behind, carrying satchels and suitcases.

Jem clutched the handles of his own worn carpetbag. He waited—eyes popping at the luxury everywhere he looked—while the family checked in. Pa handed Jem two keys. "You can head up and find our rooms if you like. Rose and I will be along in a minute."

Jem couldn't get away fast enough. He wanted out of the lobby before somebody checked under his fingernails for dirt. He snatched the keys, muttered a quick "thanks," and headed for the stairs.

Halfway up the first flight, he stumbled, caught himself, and paused. He looked at his cousin. "Do you want to go first?" He didn't explain why, but he was thinking it. *I can climb ladders, but I'm not used to so many steps all in one place.*

Nathan wasted no time taking the lead. He looked right at home, skittering up the steps with his satchel as if he'd climbed stairs all his life. Which Jem knew he had. Once, not long after he'd come to live with them, Nathan talked about his old house in Boston. Jem had listened patiently, since his cousin was especially homesick that day.

"It was two stories high, plus an attic, with a window at the very top," Nathan had related with shining eyes. "I always liked to climb up there and watch the ships sail in and out of the harbor." Then he'd sighed. There was no harbor in Goldtown.

Jem followed Nathan up the steps to the third floor and came out in the middle of a long, narrow hallway. Elaborate paintings hung on the walls between gleaming gaslight fixtures; a row of smooth wooden doors with shiny brass numbers spread out in both directions.

"Which way?" he wondered aloud. "Left or right?"

Ellie darted to the left. "Here it is!" she shouted. "Room 311. That's Aunt Rose's and mine. And look here, Jem! Your room's next door, number 309."

"Shhh!" Nathan dropped his bag and clamped a hand over Ellie's mouth. "You're not on your gold claim in the middle of nowhere," he scolded in a low, tight voice. "There are people in these rooms, and the walls are thin. Hush!"

Ellie's cheeks reddened. She peeled Nathan's fingers away from her face and stepped back. But instead of yelling at him like she usually did back home, she dropped her head. "I . . ." She gulped and looked at Jem. He nodded. "I'm sorry," she said, blinking back tears. "I didn't think."

Jem hadn't thought about it either. Now, he glanced both ways and silently counted the doors. He counted the floors in the Union Hotel and did the arithmetic. *Forty rooms! All in this one hotel!* Then he remembered that the Orleans Hotel—with probably twice as many rooms—stood right next door. Other buildings rose even higher.

There must be thousands of people in Sacramento. And now I've gotta worry about disturbing them?

A sudden wave of homesickness for rough-and-tumble Goldtown washed over Jem. In his mind, he saw Nine Toes digging yet another coyote hole in the middle of Pioneer Street. He remembered Dry Dirt McGee tunneling behind the icehouse because he'd heard a rumor about some dead miner's lost pile.

"Betcha nobody digs mining holes in *these* streets," he murmured.

Nathan looked startled. "What?"

Jem shook his head. "Nothing." Then he took a deep breath. He didn't want to admit it, but right now Nathan seemed his only chance of not looking like a fool for the next week. "Ellie and I would sure like it if you showed us how to act in the city." He turned to Ellie. "Right?"

Ellie nodded without speaking. Her cheeks were still flushed with shame.

Nathan shrugged, but he looked pleased. "Fair's fair," he said. "You broke me into gold camp life, so I'll return the favor. There's not much to it. Just remember not to get all bug-eyed when you see something new—like the chandelier. It's a dead giveaway you're a hayseed."

"The *what?*" Ellie asked.

"That fancy, cut-glass light hanging in the lobby," Nathan said.

Chandelier. Jem tucked the new word away. Not that he'd need to remember it for long. There were no chandeliers in Goldtown. Not that he knew about, anyway.

"Wear your city clothes and act like you're in church," Nathan added. "At least when you're indoors."

"Roasted rattlesnakes, Nathan! I—"

"And don't say that, either," Nathan warned. "There are no rattlesnakes in the middle of the city. Rats, yes. Rattlesnakes, no." He snickered at the look Jem gave him.

Just then, Pa and Aunt Rose rounded the corner. Jem could tell from Pa's wide grin and his aunt's horrified expression that they'd heard Ellie's yelling all the way down the stairs. Pa winked at his daughter and ruffled her hair. Slowly, her face lost its bright color.

"What are you waiting for, Son?" Pa asked. "Unlock our rooms so we can get settled. I want to get down to the water-front before dark."

Jem whooped—softly—and jammed the key into the lock.

⊰ CHAPTER 5 ⊱

Delays and Disappointments

In the end, Pa went to the waterfront alone. It seemed like everything took longer to accomplish in the city, and settling into their hotel rooms was no exception. By the time they sorted everything out, the September sun had dipped below the horizon. Pa refused to take them to the river in the dusky light. It was too dangerous, and they wouldn't see anything of interest at night, anyway.

"I'm sorry," he told them on his way out the door. "Tomorrow morning you can wander down and have a look. The river's only a couple of blocks away, just past Front Street. Steamboats will still be docked, and you'll enjoy it much more after a full stomach and a good night's sleep."

When Jem started to protest, Pa held up a hand. "We'll be here for a whole week, Son. There's plenty to do and see, especially with the State Fair going on. It's over in Capitol Park—six square blocks of animal smells, sweat, and commotion." He grinned. "You'll like it. Be patient."

"Don't forget the horse races, Pa," Jem said, brightening. "And the shooting match. Are you going to enter it?"

"I might." With a quick wave, Pa was gone, leaving Aunt Rose to hustle the children downstairs for supper in the hotel dining room. Jem remembered Nathan's advice and pretended to act like he always ate from china plates and used white linen napkins.

The hot, thick slabs of roast beef and fluffy potatoes should have tempted Jem to gobble his food and scrape his plate like a starving miner. But once he sat down, the endless stagecoach ride caught up to him. He felt so drained he could hardly keep his eyes open, let alone find the energy to chew his food.

Halfway through the meal, Jem looked across the table at Ellie. Her eyelids fluttered, and she slumped in her seat. Even Aunt Rose looked pale. She didn't scold Ellie for slouching, but instead brought the meal to a hasty close and herded them back upstairs.

With a grateful sigh, Jem shut the connecting door to Aunt Rose and Ellie's room and fell into bed next to Nathan. He woke up briefly when Pa returned. The room was dark except for a low-burning lamp on the dresser. Jem mumbled a question.

"It's been delayed and won't dock until the day after tomorrow," Pa answered in a tired voice. "Boiler problems."

The light went out, and Jem heard no more.

Squeak . . . squeak . . . thump.

Jem lay in the dirt, eyes squeezed shut. Someone kept thumping his chest, demanding he "hand it over." The highwayman. *He wants my gold!* Another thump, and the dark shadow moved closer. *I have to get away!* Jem's eyes flew open. Heart racing, he bolted upright and scooted back against the iron rods of the headboard.

He blinked. The nightmare vanished in the bright morning light. He sagged when he saw his sister sitting on the bed, peering at him with a silly smile. Anger replaced his terror. "Hang it all, Ellie! What are you doing?"

"You're hard to wake up," she said. "I had to poke you a lot. Are you gonna sleep all day? Get up." She rose to her knees and started bouncing. "You too, Nathan."

Nathan groaned and pulled a sheet over his head. It was too hot for anything else.

Jem's pounding heart returned to normal. His gold was safe; it was only a dream. He scowled at Ellie. She was still bouncing. "Go on," he said, pushing her away. His shove sent her tumbling off the bed and onto the floor.

Thud! All three froze at the sound. Ellie stood up, her eyes round with horror. Nathan lifted his head from under the sheets. "Betcha they heard *that* in the room below."

"Maybe they're sound sleepers," Jem said. "Or maybe they're gone." From the amount of light pouring in through the open window, the day was well under way.

One person for sure heard the thump. Aunt Rose walked into the boys' room and planted her hands on her hips. "What's all the ruckus in here?" she demanded. "Ellianna, I asked you to wake the boys, *not* wake the rest of the Union's guests."

"It was my fault," Jem said, jumping to Ellie's defense. For all her bluster, his little sister did not like Aunt Rose's scoldings. Jem didn't like them any better, but he was more used to them. "I pushed her off the bed for waking us."

Aunt Rose relented. "Hmm. Well, it *is* your first day in the city, and what's done is done. Just see that there is no repeat of this morning's rowdiness, do you hear?" She directed her dark, serious gaze on them all.

"Yes, ma'am," three voices echoed back.

Her good humor restored, Aunt Rose clapped her hands together, just like Miss Cheney did when she wanted her pupils' attention. "Hurry now. Get up. Matthew let you boys sleep late this morning, but the day's awasting."

Jem threw back the covers and got up. Pa's bed was

empty, and probably had been since the crack of dawn. He was always an early riser, and no wonder. With a ranch to run and a sheriff's job in town, Matt Coulter's days were full to the brim from sunrise to sunset and beyond.

Jem tried to imitate his father's zest for rising before the sun, but sometimes—especially during the winter months—he couldn't drag himself out of bed for his chores. Or for school. Today was different, though. Jem didn't feel totally rested, but a day of exploring the city lay ahead of him. He didn't want to miss another minute.

"Where did Pa go?" He crossed the room, splashed water on his face from the bowl in the corner, and rummaged around his carpetbag for a comb. He was already dressed. He'd fallen into bed last night without bothering to change into his nightshirt. What a time-saver! He wondered how many nights he could get away with it.

None, apparently. "When you boys have changed out of those wrinkled, travel-worn clothes and into something decent, we'll have breakfast," Aunt Rose said. She ignored Jem's question and hustled Ellie from the room. "Then I'll relate Matthew's plans for the day. Hurry now." She smiled and quietly shut the door behind her.

Left alone, Jem groaned.

"City clothes, remember?" Nathan said, making a face. Over the past months, Goldtown had freed Jem's cousin from his old life in Boston. He didn't look happy to be donning his Sunday-go-to-meeting clothes any more than Jem did.

Jem yanked a clean shirt and a pair of Sunday knickers from his bag. He had only the one set of good clothes, which meant he'd have to keep them clean all week. He groaned again.

Then he sniffed and wrinkled his nose. Nathan was combing hair tonic into his blond mop. Dr. Lyman's greasy concoction stank worse than the cheap whiskey Jem occasionally whiffed passing a saloon in town.

"*That* I won't do," Jem said when Nathan held out the dark, square bottle. "Not for Sacramento. Not for Aunt Rose. Not for *anybody*." Instead, he found his hat and jammed it on his head.

Jem removed his hat at breakfast, but Aunt Rose made no comment about his hair. She picked at her food and talked, while Jem shoveled down steak and eggs.

"Since it's close by, Matthew has given permission for you to see the waterfront," she finished, dabbing her mouth with a napkin. "He has no worries, so long as you stay together at all times. He told me it's safer than parts of Goldtown." She frowned. "That's not hard to believe," she added with a sniff, showing them what she thought about their rowdy mining town.

Jem wanted to shout his *hurrah*, but he knew better. He nodded respectfully and let Auntie do all the talking, which she seemed happy to do.

"He's only giving his permission because he can't take you himself today," she went on.

"Why not?" Ellie asked between mouthfuls.

Aunt Rose sipped her coffee before answering. "Since the *New World* is delayed, he felt he should take the time to speak to Wells Fargo about other, safer ways of shipping gold to San Francisco. Not this shipment, of course. Matthew has to do what Mr. Sterling asked, but if there are future gold shipments, he would like to offer other options." She sipped again.

When Aunt Rose said no more, Jem asked, "What sort of options?"

"The railroad for one," she said.

Jem nearly leaped from his chair. "The *railroad*? He's gone to look at the railroad?" Then he slumped. "Why didn't he wake me? I want to see a train engine, and maybe ride on the cars."

Aunt Rose clucked her tongue and set her cup down. "I suspect that's the reason he went alone. It's business, not pleasure. The line to Folsom is twenty-two miles. He'll be gone all day."

"But there's no railroad to Goldtown," Jem said. "What good does it do looking at a route so far away?"

Aunt Rose smiled. "Your father's thinking of the future, Jeremiah. One day, railroad tracks will crisscross this state. Why, right now the Chinese who lost their mine this summer are working on tracks that will connect California to the rest of the country." Her eyes shone at the thought of traveling back East in a handful of days rather than months aboard a sailing ship.

Jem nodded. His friend Wu Shen's relatives had been gone a long time blasting through the mountains. They'd probably be gone months—or even years—longer.

He drained his glass of milk. Tracks might cover the state some day, but not today. "When can we see the river, Auntie?" He looked at the clock in the dining room. Ten-thirty. Indeed, the day was racing by.

"You may go right after breakfast," Aunt Rose replied. "I intend to look around the shops today. I brought a list of things one can only get in the city." Her look turned serious. "I want you back here no later than two this afternoon. That's more than enough time to see every steamer at the wharf and to count each crate and barrel and stick of firewood as they're loaded. Is that clear?"

Three heads bobbed up and down.

"Nathan," Aunt Rose said, "you know your way around a waterfront. You've been to the Boston docks countless times. I expect you to keep a clear head and avoid trouble. And steer clear of the riffraff along the wharf."

Nathan's eyebrows went up, clearly surprised at the sudden change in leadership. He nodded, but flicked Jem a concerned look. Everybody knew who was usually in charge.

As much as Jem wanted to burst out that *he* was the eldest, he didn't. He always kept Nathan and Ellie out of trouble when they explored the foothills around Goldtown. He knew the dangers and how to avoid them. Along the waterfront, however, it only made sense that Nathan should take the lead.

Jem grinned. "Sounds like a good idea to me, Cousin. Now it'll be *your* job to keep Ellie from falling off the wharf and into the river."

A sharp kick from under the table told Jem what Ellie thought of his teasing. He caught her glare, which clearly read, *I can take care of myself.*

Maybe she could—in Goldtown. But not here. Not in this enormous city, where the buildings stood thick as pine trees. It would be just as easy to get lost in this brick forest as any-place in the Sierras.

Right then, Jem determined that by the end of the day he would know the wharf along the Sacramento River as well as—or better than—anybody who lived here.

⊰ CHAPTER 6 ⊱

Wharf Rats

To Aunt Rose, "right after breakfast" meant after another half hour of fussing. She marched the cousins upstairs to make sure they were smartly dressed, so as not to raise eyebrows from the city folks. She retied the ribbons in Ellie's braids, told Nathan to tuck in his shirt, and reminded Jem to keep his hat on. Then she pronounced them spick-and-span and shooed them out the door.

Jem hurried down the stairs and through the lobby, ignoring the chandelier that had awed him the evening before. Today it was just a distraction. Aunt Rose's two o'clock deadline remained firm; there was no time to gawk at every fancy bauble that caught his eye. He wanted to see the river and the steamboats, whose long, deep whistle blasts filled the air with such urgency. *Get aboard!*

"Come on," he urged Nathan and Ellie, breaking out into the bright sunshine. He blinked and pulled his wide-brimmed hat farther over his forehead. Halfway down the block to the left, he recognized the Express office. "Let's go this way."

Nathan seemed agreeable, so Jem took the lead. At first, he felt like he was right back in Goldtown, threading his way along the busy wooden sidewalk. The only difference was these folks dressed fancier. Ladies with lacy parasols glided along the boardwalk. Twice, Jem had to sidestep into the street to avoid brushing up against a full, swaying skirt.

"They're taking up the entire walk," Ellie grumbled, snatching at Jem's hand.

Jem didn't mind holding her hand. The tall buildings all looked alike. People were everywhere, bustling about. He'd teased Nathan earlier about watching out for Ellie, but Jem knew she was *his* responsibility. Pa would have his hide if anything happened to her.

Looking around, Jem saw plenty of chances for getting hurt. Sacramento's streets were wide, and choked with traffic: carriages, fast buggies, wagons, peddlers pushing handcarts, and people on horseback. Jem saw a hole in the flow, tugged on Ellie's hand, and darted across the street, hoping Nathan could follow. Without pausing to catch his breath, he led them around a corner and onto a street that pointed in the direction of the river.

"The way folks are rushing about, you'd think somebody just hit pay dirt," Jem said when they were out of harm's way. "What's the hurry? There's no gold rush here."

Nathan fell into step beside Jem. "This isn't so busy. You should see Boston on a sunny day. It's a lot more crowded. And more refined. Look"—he pointed—"this street isn't even paved."

But at least the blocks were square and straight. Pa said the streets were named for the alphabet and numbered in order. How could anybody get lost? But he kept hold of Ellie's hand, just in case, and memorized the Union Hotel's address. *Second Street, between J and K.*

Half a block later, they came to a row of barrels. A wide plank lay across the barrels, loaded down with dark bottles of all shapes and sizes. Behind the makeshift counter, a scruffy-looking man in a red vest and a long, black overcoat was waving one of the bottles in the air.

"Get your Dr. Shoops remedies right here!" he shouted above the hustle and bustle. "Guar-an-teed to cure coughs, pimples, indigestion, and nervousness."

Most bystanders kept moving. Jem didn't slow down either. He could see the same swindlers in Goldtown: Syria, the gypsy woman, who told fortunes; old Sly Eyes, with his silly bird that predicted the future by picking up bits of colored paper; "Doc" Fineas hawking his cure-all potions that didn't cure anything. All of them after only one thing: a miner's hard-earned gold.

"I seen it work on dead men and give 'em back their health and vigor . . ." The medicine man's voice faded as Jem, Nathan, and Ellie hurried past.

One block later, the riverfront opened up before them, a jumble of docks, levees, cargo, and warehouses. Trees dotted the riverbank; buildings crept nearly to the water's edge. People were everywhere.

Rising above the river, a paddle-wheel steamboat filled Jem's view. Two tall, black smokestacks rose into the sky. Smoke billowed from the flues, and a whistle blew, long and deep. It looked ready to steam away.

Ellie clapped her hands over her ears at the noise. Jem stood, his gaze transfixed on this river monster. He knew his mouth was hanging open, but he couldn't help it. What a sight!

Nathan yanked Ellie's hands away from her ears. Then he dug his elbow into Jem's side. "Close your mouth," he hissed in Jem's ear, but he might just as well have shouted. No one could hear him over the racket. "Act like you see steamers every day."

"And *you* have?" Jem asked, tearing his eyes away from the spectacle.

"I've never seen a riverboat," Nathan admitted. "But I've seen plenty of steamers and sailing ships. That little side-wheeler is nothing like a seagoing vessel. And this river is a bathtub compared to the ocean." He snorted. "No proper wharf either. Just dirt and planking for a dock."

Jem heard a teensy bit of know-it-all in his cousin's voice, but he bit his tongue to keep from snapping at him. Nathan had spent six months at sea coming to California. He *did* know it all, at least when it came to ships.

The whistle blew again, and the gangplank was hauled aboard. From a deck on the second level, passengers waved. As the steamer slid away from the riverbank, Jem saw its name on the paddle-wheel housing: *Antelope*.

He sighed. *I sure wish I was aboard.* Questions buzzed in his head. *What makes the paddles slap through the water? How do they steer her?* Jem knew every step a chunk of ore took when it was smashed in the huge stamp mill to separate the gold. But he knew nothing about ships or how they worked.

Ellie's gasp pulled Jem from his thoughts. He followed her gaze and worked hard to keep his eyes from bugging out. Paddleboats of all sizes lined the waterfront in both directions as far as Jem could see. He ran up on the levee to get a better look. With the *Antelope* no longer blocking his view, he could see more steamers chugging up and down the river, along with barges and small sailing ships.

Nathan yanked on his shirt sleeve. "You're doing it again," he teased.

Jem flushed. Then he dug his hands in his pockets and looked around. Not far away, three boys about his own age were loafing near a jumble of barrels, crates, and other cargo. They looked perfectly at home, slapping the caps off their fellows, chasing each other around the crates and firewood, and throwing rocks in the river. Jem wished he could be so casual.

A steamer whistle blew, and Jem jumped, but the other boys had paid it no mind. They jostled each other then pointed and took off, their bare feet slapping along the shoddy dock.

A block away, an especially fine side-wheeler lay docked. It looked two or three times bigger than the *Antelope*. Jem caught his breath. Everything about this steamboat shouted luxury and wealth. "That steamboat's a beauty," he told Nathan. "What do you say we see it up close?"

Nathan shook his head. "Not if you two are gonna act like hayseeds." He shaded his eyes and looked to see where the boys had gone. "I don't want to be poked fun at by those wharf rats."

"You're not my boss," Ellie said. "I'm gonna go see that steamboat."

Jem gripped Ellie's arm. "Don't be a goose. You're not going anywhere by yourself. And Nathan *is* the boss on the wharf today, remember?" He turned to Nathan just as another loud whistle blared. "See? I didn't even twitch that time. I'm getting used to the city fast."

Nathan laughed. "All right. Let's go see it." He led the way toward the glistening, white steamer.

Jem had barely read the side-wheeler's name, *River Duchess*, when he heard an all-too-familiar sound. The commotion on the docks had died down after the other ship steamed away, and Jem's ears pricked up. "Listen!"

All three whirled. The scuffling, banging, and painful grunts seemed to come from a narrow space between a stack of firewood and a small warehouse some yards away.

"It's probably those boys we saw earlier," Nathan said. He looked worried. "You know, the riffraff Mother warned us about. Most likely they're fighting over something they stole. I've seen it before. It's best to stay away. Let's head the other way."

Ellie protested, but Jem told her they'd come back later. "Nathan probably knows what he's talking about," he said.

Jem was about to turn around when a shriek of terror sent shivers up his neck. This was not the sound of ruffians taking punches at each other but the cry of a helpless victim. He'd heard it often enough in Goldtown. "They're roughing somebody up back there," he said, taking a step toward the ruckus.

"No, Jem." Nathan clutched his cousin's arm. "The boys who loaf around the docks are meaner than"—he swallowed—"meaner than a nest of rattlesnakes."

Jem pulled himself loose. "Betcha they're no meaner than some of the rowdies in a gold camp. Betcha I—" A painful wail kept the rest of Jem's words inside. He clenched his fists and darted across the dock, straight toward the source of the scuffling and bumping. "Look after Ellie!" he called over his shoulder then rounded the corner.

In the shadows, Jem recognized the barefoot boys from earlier. Two were holding a slight, well-dressed boy against the building, while a third punched and kicked him. The boy's face was bloody, his hair a mop of disheveled black waves. He flailed his fists and shrieked at his attackers in a foreign language.

"Shut up!" one of the boys ordered, hitting him. "Give the rest over, and be quick about it."

"Non, non!" The boy clutched his vest. His torn jacket lay at his feet. Tears of rage and pain dripped down his cheeks.

Rip! Half his vest tore loose. There was a pause while the biggest boy rummaged around inside the pockets.

"Leave him alone!" Jem yelled.

Startled, the boys turned as one and gaped at the stranger blocking the narrow gap.

Before they could gather their wits, Jem barreled into them. He'd had plenty of practice back in Goldtown, and he knew surprise was his best weapon. It worked. One boy went down; the others stumbled back in bewilderment.

But only for a moment. Then they were on their feet, coming at Jem like a pack of wolves deprived of their prey. They ignored the young foreign boy and focused their attention on this new intruder.

Jem saw stars when the back of his head smacked against the wood stack, and his hat flew off. He recovered quickly, though, and threw the biggest boy aside. Jem heard his Sunday shirt rip. *Uh-oh!*

There was no time to worry about a scolding. He ducked a blow to his head and sent his fist into the attacker's jaw. The boy backed off with a yelp. Jem kicked the ruffian who had him by the arm and heard a satisfying *oof.* His arm slid free.

Jem smiled between clenched teeth. He might be dressed like a city-bred gentleman, but life in Goldtown had sharpened his wits and his muscles. Growing two inches this past year hadn't hurt either. These ruffians were clearly not prepared for somebody so dressed to fight them on their own terms.

It suddenly crossed Jem's mind that Pa—and especially Aunt Rose—might not look favorably on this fight. But *roasted rattlesnakes!* How could he let these wharf rats rough up this kid? Jem's namesake, the prophet Jeremiah from the Bible, wrote about doing what was right and just, and rescuing the helpless who were getting robbed.

The boy was certainly being robbed, but he was not as helpless as Jem supposed. And a good thing too. The rowdies seemed to catch on that there was only one of Jem. They lunged for him anew. A sudden attack from behind showed Jem that the boys' victim had recovered enough to join in. He leaped on the back of the smallest attacker and began pulling his hair and yelling in what sounded to Jem like French.

Nathan's shrill, "Need help, Cousin?" turned the tide.

The bullies fell away at this new threat. The rowdy who was suffering under the French boy's piggyback ride yanked him off and slammed him to the ground. Two others ripped away the rest of his vest and snatched up his jacket. Then, spouting a stream of curses, they fled down the narrow passageway in the opposite direction of Jem and the others.

⊰ CHAPTER 7 ⊱

A New Friend

The boy at Jem's feet leaped up and waved his fist in the air. *"Vers le bas avec les intimidateurs!"* he hollered after the running forms. For an instant, it looked as if he might chase them down and give them a piece of his mind—if not his fists.

Not a good idea, Jem thought. Except for riding piggyback for ten seconds, the young victim had not helped in his rescue. He should thank Jem and Nathan for *that.* Which he did, after he spat after the bullies and watched them turn the corner.

"Merci, merci," he gushed, turning to Jem. Then he babbled on for half a minute in a torrent of French.

"Hold on!" Jem broke in. He raised his hands to back up his words, in case the boy didn't understand English. For sure, Jem didn't speak any French. He spent little time with the French miners in Goldtown. Too bad. Learning their language would have come in handy right about now. "Can you speak English?" he asked.

The boy nodded vigorously. *"Oui, oui . . .* I mean yes, I speak English." He gritted his teeth. "But those *voyous,* those evil thugs—" He broke off. "Forgive me. When I am angry or excited, I forget my English." He bowed slightly then straightened. "My name is Henri Belrose. Whom do I have the honor of thanking for my rescue?"

Jem introduced himself and Nathan. "And this is my sister, Ellie," he finished.

Ellie stepped to Jem's side. She didn't look at all happy at being left out of the action. Nathan must have had a hard time holding her back. She showed her annoyance by scowling at Jem before turning to Henri. "Howdy," she said, eyeing his bloodied face and torn shirt. "Those wharf rats really licked you good."

Henri sniffed back the still-dripping blood and swiped his shirt sleeve across his nose.

Ellie made a face. "That didn't help much."

Henri frowned. "You speak your thoughts, don't you?"

"All the time," Jem muttered. He pulled a handkerchief from his back pocket. "Here. Use this."

Henri took the cloth with a *merci* and began mopping his face.

Jem watched the boy clean himself up. He wasn't as tall as Nathan and not nearly as filled out. His slight build, pale face, and fancy getup marked him as the pampered son of rich city folks. It was true he'd shown spunk when he jumped on the bully's back, but Henri was definitely what folks in Goldtown called a *dandy*. Even Will Sterling, the mine owner's son and the richest kid in town, never dressed or looked like this.

Henri held the handkerchief out, but Jem waved it away. "Keep it." Then he asked, "What did they take?"

Henri jammed the soiled cloth into his waistband and muttered, "*Vers le bas avec les intimidateurs* . . . Down with bullies!" His fists balled at his sides. "Those . . . what did you call them? Wharf rats?"

When Ellie nodded, he grimaced. "A good name. Those

wharf rats robbed me of two double eagles and all my smaller coins." He pulled out the pockets of his fitted, black breeches. "See? Empty."

Jem whistled his astonishment. What fool would carry around twenty-dollar gold pieces on the waterfront? Then he remembered he was carrying his own small stash of gold. His hand went to his pocket to make sure it was safe.

"I carry small cash in my pant pockets, but the eagles I hid in my vest," Henri said. "How could they know that?" He sounded sincerely confused.

"How could they *not?*" Nathan blurted. "Look at you. Ruffled silk shirt, fancy pants, silk stockings, shiny black shoes. No wonder those ruffians found you an easy mark. You're dressed like a rich boy, you're not very big, and you were alone." He shook his head. "They knew, all right. And if it wasn't for my cousin, you'd most likely have been beaten and left for dead."

Henri dropped his head and took a deep, shaky breath. "*Oui,* I know that now." Then his head snapped up and he looked at Jem. "I have been an *idiot,* have I not?"

To Jem, it sounded like "ee-dee-oh," and he wasn't real sure what that meant. But "dummy" came to mind. He was about to agree when he remembered that if it wasn't for Nathan's wharf-sense, Jem might as easily find himself in the same fix. There were places in Goldtown Jem knew better than to wander near, but in this sprawling city? *I'm just as ignorant as this French boy.*

He shrugged and stuck out his hand. "You'll do," he said. "It's nice meeting you, but we better be getting back. Those rowdies might return with their big brothers."

Henri's eyes grew wide in alarm. Then he relaxed and shook Jem's hand. "Don't go," he pleaded. "I have no gold left to repay you for rescuing me from those *barbares* . . . those barbarians. But if you accompany me back to the *River*

Duchess, mon père, Captain Anton Belrose, will be pleased to reward you for your kindness, and in gold."

Jem and Nathan exchanged astonished looks. Henri's father was the captain of that big steamboat? Lucky!

Ellie sucked in a breath, and her eyes lit up. "That would be swell!"

Jem elbowed her into silence. "I don't have to be paid to follow what the Bible says about helping folks," he told Henri. "Besides, I don't need your gold. I pan my own." He glanced around, spied his hat, and plopped it on his head. "Let's get away from here and I'll show you."

Once out of the shadows, Jem opened his gold pouch and let Henri admire the mixture of flakes, dust, and small nuggets. The boy murmured in French then gaped at Jem. "So, you are a real, live gold prospector, *non?* Striking it rich? Making your pile? Hitting color? Seeing the elephant?"

"No, not really," Jem said, chuckling. Henri's odd accent made the gold-rush slang sound hilariously funny. He'd no doubt been reading plenty of dime novels. "The gold rush is about over these days." He sighed and returned his pouch to safety. "Unfortunately." He started back toward the wharf.

Henri kept in step with Jem and Nathan. "I wish I could work a pan with you alongside a river full of gold," he said.

"Good luck finding one," Nathan muttered.

Jem laughed. Last spring, his city cousin had sounded just like Henri. In the back of his mind, Jem could still hear Nathan bellowing endless verses of a silly song about pockets full of gold. It didn't take long, however, before

Nathan learned the hard truth about gold panning: It wasn't easy, and hardly anyone struck it rich.

Henri's face crumpled. "So, what you say is true? There is no gold left in the gold country?"

"There's no *easy* gold left," Jem said. "But there's still plenty of gold in the mountains. You just have to dig deep tunnels to find it."

"There's gold in the Midas mine," Ellie burst out, her voice full of pride. "More than you can shake a stick at. There's so much gold that our pa just brought down eighty-five thousand—"

Jem's hand clapped over Ellie's mouth with a loud *smack*. He didn't say a word, but his glare spoke volumes. *You keep a lid on Pa's business!*

Ellie, who could usually guess what her brother was thinking, had no trouble now. Her hazel eyes looked scared. She clearly realized her mistake, and nodded.

Jem removed his hand. *"Girls,"* he told Henri with a nervous laugh. "Worse than chipmunks chattering, and you can never make sense of anything they say. Don't pay her no mind." He brushed Ellie's words away and changed the subject. "You got any sisters?"

Ellie's cheeks blazed at Jem's words, but she kept quiet.

"Three," Henri said, sighing. "All younger than I, and constantly wanting me to entertain them. I think *Maman* finally realized I needed time for myself. In honor of my twelfth birthday, she agreed I should accompany *Papa* aboard the *Duchess*. It is my first trip upriver since we left New Orleans two years ago."

That explains a lot, Jem thought. Henri had probably never wandered alone along a riverfront in his life. Judging by what he saw, Henri's mother probably didn't let him out of her sight. Jem cringed. Worse than Aunt Rose!

"If *Maman* saw me now," Henri said, "this would also be

my last trip to the 'wild, untamed frontier,' as she calls it." He brushed at the rusty-red streaks on his sleeves. "It is good that she stayed in San Francisco."

"Sacramento—the wild, untamed frontier?" Jem laughed. "This is the biggest city I've ever seen. I had to ask my Boston cousin"—he elbowed Nathan and grinned—"to look out for me so I don't end up acting like a yokel from the hills."

By now, the group had returned to the planking along the riverfront. Ellie hadn't said a word since Jem lit into her, and he began to relax. Henri seemed distracted from the subject of gold. He was prattling on about his old life in the French Quarter of New Orleans.

"New Orleans is *huge*," Henri was saying. "And very refined." His eyes darkened. "It is a shame what those *barbare* Yankees are doing to my city, and to the entire South. That is why *mon père* had to take one of his steamboats and come here. It is no longer safe for him to navigate the Mississippi. But one day, when this War of Northern Aggression is over, we will return home. *Papa* promised *Maman*."

Jem said nothing. It felt as if a dark cloud had suddenly settled over the group. Nathan licked his lips and looked at him. Jem felt his stomach lurch. Henri's father was a Confederate. Which put Henri on the wrong side of the war.

Not far away, the *River Duchess* loomed, blocking the view of the river. There was no sign of the rowdies. Jem shifted uncomfortably. It was probably best to say good-bye and head back to the hotel. Nothing good could come from going around with this new boy. Not when the Knights of the Golden Circle had robbed the stage. Not with Ellie's near-blunder about the gold for the Union.

At the awkward silence, Henri wrinkled his dark brows. "What did I say?" Then his eyes widened and he looked at Nathan. "Oh . . . you are from Boston. A Yankee." He sounded embarrassed. "And you too?" he asked Jem.

58

Jem had never considered the question. He thought of himself as a Californian. The States and the war were far away. But apparently not far enough. He nodded.

Henri sighed. "Forgive me. I spoke without thinking. San Francisco is full of Southerners, so I just assumed you . . ." His voice trailed off and he shrugged. "Had you known I'm from the South, would you have come to my aid?"

"Of course," Jem answered quickly. "Where I come from, if somebody's in trouble, you help him first and sort out your differences later."

Henri's smile returned. "*Merci.* We are still friends, then?"

Jem paused. Maybe he shouldn't brush the French boy off so quickly, just because he'd blurted his thoughts. *I've done that plenty of times.* Henri had showed a lot of character by apologizing. Jem wasn't sure he'd have been so quick to admit his faults.

"Sure," he decided with a shrug. "Why not? After all, it's the grown-ups' war."

"*Oui*, I agree. And now, I must insist that you allow me to repay you for your kindness."

"No," Jem said. "You don't have to. Really, we—"

"Would you like to see the *River Duchess*?"

Jem's polite refusal died away. He swallowed his surprise and stared at Henri. He heard Ellie catch her breath.

"Have you ever been aboard a steamboat?" Henri asked.

Jem slowly shook his head.

"I didn't think so," Henri said with a merry laugh. "Come, and I will show you the best steamer on the Sacramento River." He waved to include Nathan and Ellie. "You may *all* come."

Eagerness to see the riverboat made Jem's heart race, just as if he'd struck it rich when he least expected it. How could he say no to a tour of the *River Duchess*?

He couldn't.

⊰ CHAPTER 8 ⊱

The River Duchess

When Jem agreed to a "real quick" tour of the side-wheeler, Ellie let out a whoop and clapped her hands. He knew she was on pins and needles waiting for his answer. She'd kept quiet, but she'd no doubt been praying that her big brother would accept Henri Belrose's offer.

A glance at the sun told Jem they were running out of time. "We only have about an hour," he said.

"That is time enough to see everything," Henri assured them.

"It better be," Jem said. "We just got here, and the river-front's not the only place I want to see. If we're late getting back"—he made a slashing motion across his neck—"Aunt Rose will keep us on a short leash for the rest of the week."

Nathan's grim nod backed Jem up.

With Pa gone for the day, Aunt Rose was in charge, and Jem did *not* want to cross her. It was different in Goldtown, where he knew every hill, creek, and mining hole. Months ago, Pa had convinced his older sister to let the cousins run free.

But the rules were not the same here in the city.

Henri waved Jem's concerns away. "Do not worry. If for

some reason you cannot see everything now, you can always return another—" He broke off and sighed. "No, that will not be possible. The *Duchess* is scheduled to depart at first light tomorrow." He pointed toward his father's steamer. "They have been hauling cargo aboard since sunup."

Jem looked around. The dock was piled high with goods and cordwood. Freight wagons crowded around with more cargo waiting to be loaded. Dockworkers tipped barrels onto their sides and rolled them along the gangplank.

Jem looked around in astonishment. "All this is going to fit on that boat?"

Henri nodded. "And more. Plus the wood for the boilers." He pointed to the wide-open lower deck. "Right now it's nearly empty, but it will soon be stacked wherever there's room. The more freight *Papa* can cram in the cargo hold and on deck, the more money he will make when we arrive in San Francisco. We have passengers too. Wealthy people fill the staterooms, and the rest crowd onto the deck. The *Duchess* can hold close to three hundred." He nudged Jem. "Come on. I will take you aboard."

Jem was suddenly not so sure. The short, grizzled man shouting from his spot next to the gangplank looked unwelcoming. His words to the dockworkers and deckhands were quick, sharp, and sprinkled with threats and curses. Another man stood next to him, his pen poised over a book.

"Mr. Benz, the clerk, is holding the ledger," Henri explained. "He's checking off cargo as it comes aboard. The shouting man is the first mate, Mr. Peasley. He is in charge of the crew. He expects the cargo to be placed just so, *or else.*" Henri made a face. "He is very bad-tempered. I try to stay away from him."

"How do you expect us to get past him?" Nathan asked.

Henri shook his head. "You can't. Peasley would allow *me* to board, of course, but not you three. I would have to find *Papa* and explain the whole story before you could come aboard." He shrugged. "That would take too much time."

"Then how—" Jem began.

"There are more ways to board the *Duchess* than by using the gangplank," Henri said with a grin. When Jem hesitated, the French boy urged him on. "*Mon père* will be pleased when he learns how you rescued me today. He will welcome you aboard, I promise. After I show you around, I will take you up to the pilothouse and introduce you. Don't worry."

Jem couldn't argue with Henri's reasoning. The chance to go aboard the *River Duchess* made him tingle all over. After today, the paddleboat would be long gone, and Jem would probably never get another opportunity.

"The worst that ol' first mate can do is kick us off the boat," Ellie piped up. "I say we get aboard any way we can."

"*Bravo!*" Henri said. "Follow me."

Jem and the others stayed close on their guide's heels as he ran along the wharf, away from the front of the ship and Mr. Peasley's sharp eyes. Henri dodged a stack of crates and led them past the tall, wooden structure that housed the paddle wheel. It rose at least thirty feet above them. The name "River Duchess" was painted on the side in bold, black letters. Jem craned his neck and gawked as he hurried by.

Just beyond the housing, close to the stern, Henri stopped. Then he backed up, took a running leap, and sailed across the narrow gap of water between the wharf and the ship.

Jem caught his breath at the boy's daring. True, Jem had jumped wider mining holes back home, but if he missed this time, the river was there, waiting to soak him.

"It's easy," Henri said. "Hurry!"

Jem took a good look before he leaped. The waist-high railings he'd seen farther forward were missing back here, and this part of the boat's deck sat nearly level with the wharf. It didn't take much to figure out that as soon as the hold was full of cargo, the deck would rest even lower, until it sat on top of the water almost like a raft.

I can do this, Jem decided, backing up. He ran and jumped. Nathan was only a footstep behind. *Thump . . . thump.* Two sets of boots landed on the wooden deck of the *River Duchess.*

Ellie's legs were not as long as the boys. She leaped but didn't quite make it. Her feet touched the edge of the boat then slipped out from under her. With a yelp, she came down hard on the deck and began to slide over the edge.

"Help!" she squeaked. "I'm slipping!" Her fingers scrambled to find a handhold. Jem threw himself down next to Ellie and caught her arms. With Nathan's help, he hauled her aboard. When he saw his sister's dripping shoes, Jem's stomach turned over. If they hadn't caught her in time, she would have taken a serious dunking—and neither he nor Ellie could swim.

Ellie sloshed around in her shoes and grinned. Nothing ever troubled her for long. "That was a mighty close call, but I'm fine."

"It was too close for my liking," Jem said, snagging her hand. "You stay with me."

"Let's go," Henri said. He ducked around the paddle-wheel housing and waved Jem and the others to follow.

When no one yelled or no whistle blew an alarm, the thrill of delight replaced Jem's earlier panic. *I'm really here! I'm aboard a steamboat!* He gripped Ellie's hand tighter. The *Duchess* was huge. It would not be wise to let his sister fall behind or get lost.

"This is the cargo deck," Henri told them. "It holds the boilers, firewood, cargo, and the crew quarters." He pointed to a large, square hole in the middle of the stern deck. "That leads to the cargo hold. Most of the freight is stowed below. It runs the length of the ship. Want to see it?"

Jem glanced down the narrow steps into the dark hole. He heard thumping and cursing. The deck crew were loading freight, and Jem didn't want to get in their way. He shook his head and straightened up.

"It's cramped down there," Henri agreed. "Come on." A narrow passageway led to the crew quarters, and he let them peek inside.

Ellie held her nose at the stench of unwashed bodies in small compartments, but Jem shoved it away. "Don't be rude," he whispered in her ear. "It doesn't smell any worse than the miners after a day underground."

The boilers took up a good chunk of the engine room on the cargo deck. It took a lot of steam to run the two paddle wheels—one on either side of the steamboat. The black metal tanks were surrounded by tubing and gauges. The firebox looked big enough to hold a whole forest of wood.

"A big fire inside a wooden ship," Jem mused aloud. "Sounds dangerous to me."

"That it is, laddie!" A loud voice brought all four of them around. "Henri, lad, what're you doing hanging around my boilers?" He stepped up and ruffled Henri's black waves none too gently.

"This boy saved me from a bad beating, Kelly," Henri said, ducking away from the brawny, red-cheeked man. "And he chased some robbing wharf rats away."

"Did he indeed?" Kelly gave Jem an approving look then narrowed his eyes at Henri's missing jacket and rumpled, blood-stained shirt. "The docks are no place for you, lad. Where was Silas? I heard your father warn you just this morning that if you went ashore, you must take along—"

"Silas is the cabin boy, not my nanny," Henri interrupted with a scowl. "I left him behind so he could not shadow me." Then his look turned merry. "In return for helping me, I promised my new friend a look at the *Duchess*. May I show him your boilers?"

Kelly pulled on his lip then grunted. "Make it quick, then off you go. I don't want the captain calling down the tube, wondering why my engines lie idle." He stepped aside and let the group admire his boilers.

Henri pointed out the gadgets and explained how they made the mighty ship run. "I spend a lot of time down here with Kelly. He tells me many things about boilers and steam engines."

Kelly crossed his thick arms and nodded soberly. "Boilers are tricky things. Even a steady hand and watchful eye like my own don't always keep 'em from exploding." The engineer scratched his chin. "I recall not too long ago, just downriver from here, the *Washoe* blew her boiler." He shook his head. "Frightful loss of life. And before that, there—"

"Like you said," Henri broke in, "you have work to do, and I have a steamboat to show off."

Kelly winked. "Get along with you then. The *Duchess* is worth looking at, to be sure." He waved them out of his space and hollered at two crewmen nearby to get off their duffs and back to work.

Jem followed Henri, shaking his head. It looked like Engineer Kelly and his men had their work cut out for them, keeping a fire blazing day and night. "I reckon a fire aboard a wooden boat doesn't sound any crazier than a fire near the supporting beams of a mine," Jem remarked when they passed through the rest of the lower deck.

Henri shrugged. "*Mon père* says life is a risk. But without this risk, we would starve to death, *non?* Steamships are our family's livelihood."

Jem was forced to agree. The miners lit candles and kerosene lamps underground all the time. That was *their* livelihood. At least once a week, the mine's whistle blew, sending fear into the hearts of loved ones. Most of the time the warning meant an injury, but occasionally . . .

Jem shook himself free from the dreadful memory of being caught in a mine cave-in. The Midas's whistle had surely blown for him and his friends the night they lay trapped underground. All of a sudden, a steamboat sounded a lot safer than a mine.

"All right?"

Jem flinched at Henri's question. He hadn't been listening. "I'm sorry. What?"

"I said we should stay away from the bow of the ship, where Mr. Peasley is overseeing the loading. He would like nothing better than to toss you three in the river and drag me to *Papa*. I would rather see *mon père* on my own terms—not on Peasley's."

"Oh, right," Jem quickly agreed.

The cousins followed Henri up a narrow stairway and onto the next deck.

"This is the boiler deck," Henri said. "Staterooms for the well-to-do passengers, washrooms, a bar, and the dining room. Take a look." He led them through the long, richly furnished dining area and out the other end. Four black-skinned young men dressed in white were setting things in order for the upcoming trip. Other than the cabin crew, the place was deserted.

Jem whistled. "This dining room's bigger and fancier than the Union Hotel's restaurant. There's even . . . *chandeliers*." He felt pretty good for remembering the name of those hanging lights.

Henri waved them on. "The pantry's down this way." He pointed aft, along the outside deck. "It's where we keep the stores." He turned and hung over the deck railing. "A nice view, *non?*"

Jem nodded and gaped at the scene. The Sacramento waterfront and the streets leading toward the main part of the city looked as busy as an anthill.

"The view gets better from higher up," Henri said. "Come on."

Another stairway, more narrow passages, and more staterooms. "And quarters for the officers." He threw open a door to a tiny room. "This is my cabin."

Jem looked around. It was not much bigger than a cubbyhole, with a bunk, a small stand with a pitcher and bowl, some hooks, and a shelf for books. A chest sat snuggly under a small window, where Henri most likely kept his clothes.

By the time Henri finished showing them around, Jem was ready to admit that the French boy must be the luckiest kid in California. He gripped the deck railing and looked west, across the Sacramento River. "How much does it cost?"

"How much does what cost?"

"A ticket to travel aboard the *River Duchess*." Jem thrust a hand in his pocket and fingered his gold pouch.

Henri wrinkled his brow. "You wish to go to San Francisco?"

"No. But maybe I could make a quick trip to one of the landings downriver."

Henri shrugged. "It costs from twenty-five to seventy-five cents a mile—depending on what size cabin you want, or if you are a deck passenger." He looked Jem up and down. "But sometimes the captain lets strong young men exchange their passage for work. Can you help Kelly stoke the firebox? Or mop floors? Or do piles and piles of dishes?"

"Sure I could," Jem said before Nathan or Ellie could chime in. "If Pa says so. And if your father agrees."

Henri swung away from the deck railing and pointed. "Up there is the pilothouse. You can just see the top of it from here. *Papa* will be there. You can ask him. Come. It's getting late."

Jem glanced up at the sun. The hour had flown by! He fell in behind Henri and hurried up the last staircase and onto the steamer's highest deck. There were no railings here, but only a flat rooftop. Four or five short steps led up to the pilothouse, which sat perched in the center of the deck. Henri led the cousins, pointing out the large windows that lined all four sides. "From up here, the pilot navigates the river," he said. "He watches for snags and other dangers."

Jem felt like he was standing on top of the world. The entire city of Sacramento spread out before him. He'd stood on mountain tops before, but all he could see then were trees and more mountains. But here—

The sound of sharp voices yanked Jem back. Inside the pilothouse, three men were in a deep, angry discussion. They hadn't noticed the visitors. The tall man in uniform was probably Henri's father, but Jem had no idea who the other two were. The ship's master was yelling.

"Imbécile! Idiot!" The heated words pierced the thin walls like gunshots. "How could you lose the gold?"

The other man cursed. "Listen, Belrose, it wasn't our—"

Jem crouched below the windows and yanked Ellie down with him. "Your father looks busy," he told Henri. "Let's go." He didn't want to hear any more. Bad things always happened when men argued about gold—fist fights, knife fights, gunfights. He'd seen his share of that in Goldtown. It was time to leave.

"Hey!" a deep voice called from across the rooftop deck. "What are you kids doing, sneaking around up here?"

Icy prickles crept up Jem's spine. The voice sounded vaguely familiar. He spun around and caught his breath.

It was Black Boots.

CHAPTER 9

Caught!

There was no mistake. Jem recognized the shiny, black, knee-high boots and brown overcoat. He remembered the voice. Worse, he knew those steel-gray eyes. They're all Jem had seen of the man's face, but he would never forget them.

The bandit stood at the top of the steps—the only way on or off this level—blocking their escape. He didn't move. Neither did Jem. A cold, hard knot settled in Jem's stomach and set it churning. Was it only yesterday when this highwayman had robbed and terrorized their stagecoach? What was he doing *here*?

Black Boots quickly closed the distance between the deck stairs and the pilothouse. From inside, the arguing grew louder. A stream of angry French made Henri cringe.

"Answer me," Black Boots demanded, scanning the group. "Why are you kids sneaking around up—" He broke off with a startled gasp when his gaze fell on Ellie. "It's *you!*" He narrowed his eyes and rubbed his shin in clear memory of the day before.

"We are not s-sneaking around," Henri stammered. "My father is the shipmaster—Captain Belrose." He took a deep breath and his voice steadied. "These are my friends. I am showing them the ship. What is your business here, *monsieur?*"

"None of *your* business, youngster. But I must say, you have a poor choice of friends." He brushed past Henri and yanked Jem to his feet. "Since I see you with the girl, you and he"—he jerked his chin in Nathan's direction—"must be her brothers. That makes the sheriff your father. He really fixed it for us, boy. A neat little trick that will not go unpunished." He leaned closer. "Where is our gold?"

It's not yours! Jem nearly shouted, but he clamped his mouth shut. The Union gold was safe, at least as safe as it could be in this city. Nobody would rob the Wells Fargo Express office, not with the men they'd hired to protect the shipment. He relaxed.

"What gold?" Henri asked, frowning. Then his dark eyes lit up. "Oh . . . *that* gold." He glanced at Ellie.

Black Boots released Jem and turned on Henri. "So, they boasted to you, eh, young Belrose? How the sheriff was bringing down eighty-five thousand dollars' worth of gold bullion from the mines? How it is bound for the Yankees?" He let out a breath. "What kind of Confederate *are* you, boy? Did they tell you where it is, or if it's been secured aboard a ship yet?"

Henri reddened. "I know nothing of any gold. But even if I did I would not tell *you*. I don't know you. Now"—he shoved past Black Boots—"stand aside. I want to see my father."

Jem's respect for his new friend soared. Henri might fear the ruffians who roamed the wharf, but he appeared bold and confident aboard his father's ship.

Jem's thoughts were buzzing too loudly to be afraid either. *The highwaymen are here. On this ship!* Were the men in the pilothouse arguing about the Goldtown shipment? Was Captain Belrose one of those Knights of the Golden Circle, like Black Boots?

He swallowed. *I have to tell Pa they're here. And it sounds like they are still determined to get the gold.* He grabbed Ellie's hand

and shuffled away from the pilothouse. A few more feet and he could—

Black Boots reached past Henri and clamped down on Jem's arm. "Yes, let's *all* go see the good captain." He herded the kids up the short steps, opened the door, and shoved them all inside. "Look what I found, Marcus," he called to the shortest of the three men. "Our friends from yesterday."

Jem caught his breath. Marcus was the curly-haired bandit who had poked his pistol through the stagecoach window. He stood next to an enormous steering wheel near the front windows. Half the wheel rose past Jem's shoulders. The bottom half lay hidden beneath the floorboards.

"Papa!" Henri broke loose from the group and tore across the pilothouse to his father. A flurry of indignant French poured from his mouth. Jem's eyebrows rose. How could anybody talk that fast?

Ellie snickered, but Jem knew she was frightened. She didn't let go of his hand, and he could feel her fingers trembling. He glanced around, looking for another exit. Perhaps he could shove Ellie out and give her a head start. She was quick and clever, and slippery as the rocks in Cripple Creek. If anybody could get away, she could.

By the time Henri finished telling his tale, Jem had surveyed the entire pilothouse. It was a spacious chamber, richly furnished. A cushioned bench with a high back sat close to a potbellied stove. The bells were bright brass knobs, and loops of rope hung down to blow the whistles. A table covered with charts and maps was braced against one wall.

Jem did not find what he was looking for. A single door led in or out, and Black Boots stood blocking it. There was no way Jem could sneak Ellie around him.

They were trapped.

Then Captain Belrose spoke, and Jem sagged in relief at his words. "I am grateful for the aid you gave my son, young

Caught!

man." He squeezed Henri and smiled at Jem. "His clothing is in a frightful state, which proves he was not exaggerating his peril. *Merci*."

"You're welcome," Jem replied simply. He hoped the captain would now escort them off his boat. Quickly. He opened his mouth to ask, but Captain Belrose had more to say.

"Henri tells me you are not interested in a reward for your services," he said, clearly astonished. "You want only to see the *Duchess*. This is true?"

Jem nodded, but he was only half listening. His gaze flicked to Black Boots and the curly-haired bandit. They looked fidgety, their faces dark with annoyance. It wouldn't be long before one of them broke in.

"Jem would like to take passage aboard the *Duchess*," Henri blurted. "He wants to work his way downriver to one of the landings."

Not anymore! Jem shook his head. "The *Duchess* is a swell steamboat, sir, but I doubt Pa will let me ride aboard her, especially since you're leaving so soon." His grip on Ellie's hand felt slick with sweat. "Thank you, but we need to be getting back to the hotel." *And the sooner, the better.*

"By all means," Captain Belrose agreed. "Henri will accompany you. Take them by the kitchen, Henri, and have the cook give them some pastries."

Jem's stomach rumbled. Breakfast was long past, and they'd missed lunch.

The captain smiled. "It is the least I can offer to repay—"

"No, Anton," Black Boots interrupted. He crossed the room and stood at the captain's side. "These kids aren't going anywhere. At least not yet."

Captain Belrose's dark brows rose. "Why not? We have urgent business to talk over. The sooner this interruption is taken care of, the quicker we can return to our *discussion*." His eyes glinted dangerously, and Jem shivered. The Goldtown shipment and how to secure it was most likely the topic.

Henri's father might not stay friendly when he learns the truth, Jem thought. He glanced toward the now-open doorway.

"Clay can tell you that losing the gold was not our fault," Marcus insisted between clenched teeth. "The sheriff guarding the shipment switched it for worthless lead. He must have hidden the gold somewhere else in the coach."

Captain Belrose looked startled. "What has this to do with these children?"

Black Boots—*no, Clay*, Jem corrected—reached out and grabbed Ellie. Her hand slid from Jem's slippery hold before he could blink. "This girl's father is the sheriff, and the boys are probably related too," Clay explained. "As long as we have them, we can learn where the gold is and perhaps figure out a way to—"

"I'll tell you where the gold is right now," Jem said, "as soon as you let my sister go." Sweat no longer coated only his hands. Small drops trickled down from under his hat, dotting his forehead. The pilothouse sizzled in the afternoon heat, but Jem felt clammy with fear.

Clay loosened his grip on Ellie but didn't let go. "Talk, boy."

"It's in the safe at the Express office," Jem said, meeting Ellie's gaze. *Please, God! Ellie can outguess me nine times out of ten. Let her figure out what I'm thinking right now.*

He gave a short, nervous laugh. "Go ahead and try to rob Wells Fargo. It'll take more than a scruffy band of highwaymen, no matter what you call yourselves. It'll take the whole Rebel *army!*" He yanked off his hat and hurled it in Clay's face. "Run, Ellie!"

Ellie had clearly been waiting for just such a diversion. As quick as a striking rattlesnake, she bit Clay's hand, kicked him in the shin, and fled through the open doorway.

Jem knew he should wait for Nathan, but his main concern was making sure Ellie got safely off the steamboat. Nathan would have to take care of himself and make his own escape.

Jem darted out of the pilothouse and didn't bother with the steps. He leaped over them and landed on the rooftop deck with a grunt. Pain shot through his ankle. He collapsed and tried to catch his breath.

Looking around, he caught sight of Ellie racing toward the stairway. When she reached the steps, she paused and turned around. Then she swiped at her eyes and took a step toward Jem.

"No!" He stood and staggered a few steps. "Don't stop! Get off the ship. Then run as fast as you can back to the hotel. Don't wait for me. I'll catch up." When she hesitated, he yelled, *"Go!"*

Ellie whirled and disappeared down the stairs.

Jem mentally pictured the decks Ellie needed to navigate in order to reach the lowest level. She would have to weave her way through narrow passageways and past identical-looking rooms without being caught. She had a head start, but it wouldn't be long before the alarm was raised. There was surely a way for the captain to talk to the rest of the ship from the pilothouse. Engineer Kelly had mentioned a talking tube.

Then another thought hit him. Could Ellie make the jump from ship to shore without landing in the water? Jem sincerely hoped so, but he didn't have time to worry about that right now. He had troubles of his own. Sucking in a painful breath, he hurried across the deck as fast as his twisted ankle would let him.

"Kid, when I catch you, you're going to be sorry!" Clay shouted and burst from the pilothouse. Not a hint of the polite, southern gentleman from yesterday softened his words. He looked and sounded exactly like the outlaw he was. From behind Clay, Jem heard scuffling, banging, and screeching. He hoped Nathan was making good his escape.

Clay ignored the steps and jumped, landing on both feet. He charged after Jem.

Jem whirled and hobbled for the stairs. Halfway there, he heard the clatter of feet on metal steps coming up. Jem panicked. Up here he was fully in view. He had to get to a real deck, with lots of hiding places, where he could catch his breath and think things through.

His gaze skimmed the roof's edge. The deck below held plenty of nooks and crannies to lose his pursuers. The snag was in getting there. With Clay just steps behind him, and other men coming up the stairs toward him, there was only one way off this rooftop trap.

Jem ran to the edge and fell to his knees. No deck railings stood in his way up here. He rolled over onto his stomach, grabbed hold, and slid feet first over the ledge. *Let me land safely, God!* he prayed.

Then he closed his eyes, took a deep breath, and let go.

ᅴ CHAPTER 10 ᅧ

The Chase Is On

The drop was higher than Jem expected. With a startled cry, he landed hard on the deck. His twisted ankle screamed a protest, and his legs shot out from under him. He flipped headfirst into the deck railing. Blinking back tears of pain, he realized a sore head was better than the alternative. His clumsy tumble had nearly propelled him over the edge and down to the next deck.

Jem looked up. Black Boots had vanished, no doubt headed for the stairs. Apparently, only a fool kid would jump off a roof. "No, just a desperate one," Jem told himself. Using the railing for support, he heaved himself to his feet and took a deep, steadying breath. His knees felt shaky, but he couldn't rest. He limped into a narrow passageway that ran the length of the deck, wincing at each step.

What else is up here? He tried to remember the places Henri had showed him. Fancy staterooms, officer quarters, storage compartments, a few washrooms—

"He's on this deck," Clay's voice echoed from up ahead. "And he's got to be hurting. He fell pretty hard." A pause. "You, Marcus, search fore. I'll go aft. He can't get far."

Jem's heart pounded until it threatened to explode

through his chest. He stumbled through the first door he came to. A storage closet. Mops, buckets, and shelves full of scrub brushes and boxes of soap lined the tiny compartment's walls. Shutting the door, Jem felt his way through the dark and crouched in a corner. He wrapped his shaking arms around his legs and pulled them up to his chin, listening for the slightest sound.

Running feet and angry curses made Jem hold his breath. When the footsteps passed by his hiding place, he let out his breath and relaxed. Maybe he was safe for the moment. He was in no hurry to leave. His left ankle throbbed, his back hurt, and his head felt like a blacksmith had taken a hammer to it.

"But I can't stay here," he whispered into the darkness. He had to catch up with Ellie. She was probably wondering what had happened to him.

Concern for Nathan also welled up inside Jem. His cousin might still be trapped in the pilothouse with Captain Belrose, who certainly must know everything by now. If the captain was part of the Knights of the Golden Circle, would he let his only tie to eighty-five thousand dollars' worth of gold slip through his fingers? How desperate was the South to get ahold of the gold? And what about Henri? Once he learned the whole story, would he abandon Jem and the others?

By the time Jem finished thinking, he felt limp as a worn rag. The spurt of adrenaline that carried him over the roof's edge and into hiding had drained away. But his headache was gone, and the pain in his ankle had faded to a dull ache, easy to overlook. He heard no more running feet in the passageway, or any other sounds.

"They've probably given up," Jem decided hopefully. "After all, we're just kids. Even if we wanted to, we couldn't get the gold for them." He smiled at his reasoning. "They're just angry about being tricked, and taking it out on us. That's all. There's nothing they can *really* do."

Heartened by the idea that it was all—as Aunt Rose would say—a tempest in a teapot, Jem uncurled himself and rose stiffly to his feet. He winced at the first step but felt his way through the closet without limping. Cracking the door, he poked his head out and peeked up and down the narrow corridor. All appeared empty and quiet.

Ever watchful, Jem backtracked the way Henri had taken them earlier that afternoon. Each clunk or rattle sent Jem scurrying into a corner, where he held his breath, sent up a prayer, and waited. What seemed like hours later, he tiptoed down to the boiler level and ducked behind the staircase.

One more deck to go. At this rate, he would return to the hotel so late that Aunt Rose would skin him up one side and down the other. "Ellie," he whispered, "I sure hope you smooth things over with Auntie for me." He really did want to see the fair this week, and the railroad depot, and—

Jem stiffened when someone plucked his shirt sleeve. He clenched his fists and spun around, ready to punch Clay or Marcus or even Captain Belrose to get away. Then his mouth fell open, and his hands went slack. *"Henri!"*

Henri pressed a finger to his lips and motioned Jem to follow. Questions about Ellie and Nathan popped into Jem's head, but Henri gave him no chance to ask them. Darting back up the stairs and through the corridors, he led Jem into his tiny quarters. Quickly, he shut the door and collapsed onto his bunk.

Jem crumpled to the floor and lay still. It felt good to let his twisted gut unravel for a few minutes in the safety of his friend's cabin, but he couldn't stay. He had to make sure Ellie and Nathan were all right.

Henri rolled over onto his side and propped his head

up in his hand. "This is awfully exciting, don't you think? A merry chase aboard—"

"Finding a gold strike is exciting," Jem cut in angrily. "This is just plain scary . . . sort of like what you faced with those rowdies today. Was *that* exciting?" He shook his head. "I just want to find my family and go home. Where's Nathan?"

Henri sat up and swung his feet over the side of his small bunk. He bit his lip, clearly ashamed of his hasty words. "I'm sorry. I did not mean to make light of it. But don't worry. By now, Nathan is probably back at your hotel. Those men yelled all kinds of nonsense at *Papa* then banged around the pilothouse before chasing after you and your sister. As soon as they left, I showed Nathan another way off the *Duchess.*"

Jem brightened. "Your father let Nathan leave?"

"Of course," Henri said. Then he sobered. "Actually, everything happened so fast that *Papa* did not notice when Nathan and I slipped out. He was calling down the tube. I did not wait to hear what he was saying."

"What about Ellie? Did she get safely off the ship too?"

Henri shook his head. "I don't know. I have not seen her. But she seems quick and smart. I am sure she is all right."

Jem slowly sat up. "I have to find her and make sure."

"Why are you so troubled?" Henri asked. "You were never in any real danger. My father would not harm you, nor would he allow anyone else on his ship to harm you. He is a gentleman, and his word is law aboard the *Duchess.*"

"Black Boots looked pretty serious," Jem said. A shiver went through him. "He and his *gentlemen* Knights robbed us once already. And they're angrier than a nest of hornets because Pa tricked them."

"I don't understand," Henri said.

Jem took a deep breath and quickly related everything that had happened on the stagecoach trip and what the bandits called themselves and why. Henri's eyebrows lifted higher and higher, until they disappeared under his mop of wavy, black hair.

"*Je ne savais pas,*" he muttered, shaking his head.

"Huh?"

"I did not know," Henri repeated in English. "No wonder you ran away. But my father is no highwayman, and those others have left the ship. You are no longer in danger."

At Henri's words, Jem relaxed a tiny bit. If what the French boy said was true—that he'd seen Nathan off the *Duchess*—then his cousin had surely found Ellie by now. They were probably just as worried about him as he was about them. He needed to get back.

However, a question had been smoldering inside Jem ever since he'd heard the argument in the pilothouse, and now he blurted it out. "Henri, is your father one of those Knights of the Golden Circle?"

Henri ducked his head. When he looked up, two spots of red colored his cheeks. He nodded. "The Knights are honorable men. I cannot believe they would act like bandits."

"You *better* believe it. They still want that gold shipment to send to the South."

Henri left his bunk and joined Jem on the floor. "It is true that *Papa* loves the South, and we all miss New Orleans dreadfully. *Maman* hates San Francisco. It is cold, wet, and foggy, even in the summertime. Her only joy comes from visiting other Southern families who live there." He shook his head. "But they would never do anything so shameful as stealing."

"Maybe not for themselves," Jem said. "But what about for their cause?"

Jem's words threw Henri into silence. He frowned, drummed his fingers on his leg, and looked deep in thought. Jem was thinking hard too. Pa had kept the Goldtown shipment a secret from him. It was likely the captain was keeping a bigger secret from Henri.

Finally, Henri stood up. "Come with me. I will take you to *Papa*. He will assure you that all is well."

Jem sprang to his feet, ignoring the twitch in his ankle. "No thanks! Just show me the way off this boat, and I'll get out of your father's hair." Captain Belrose might be everything his son boasted, but he was also a Knight of the Golden Circle. Jem was not about to take any risky chances.

Henri looked hurt. He shrugged, crossed the cramped room, and flung open the door. "Follow me," he said. "You are in no danger from those two highwaymen, but if First Mate Peasley sees you, he'll scream 'stowaway' and haul you to the captain anyway."

So, instead of boldly marching down the gangplank in front of the crew, Henri took Jem the way they'd come aboard earlier. They clattered down the two flights of stairs and skirted around the engine room. It hummed with preparations for firing up the boilers and getting under way.

Near the paddle-wheel housing, Henri thrust out his hand. "Thank you again, Jem, for rescuing me from those wharf rats. Are we still friends, even though your tour of the *Duchess* was cut short by unprincipled scoundrels?"

Jem shook the French boy's hand and laughed. Henri sure talked funny, especially with his odd accent. "Yes, we're still friends. And I liked the tour. If you ever get a chance to visit Goldtown, I'll ask my friend Will to show you his father's mine. Your eyes will bug out at such a sight."

Henry's eyes grew huge right then. "You would do such a thing for me?"

Jem dropped his hand and looked toward shore. "Come to Goldtown and you'll see." Then he backed up to take his run. "Have a good trip downriver tomorrow." He ran across the deck and leaped ashore.

When his feet hit the ground, Jem kept running. He ignored the pain in his ankle and wasted no time lingering on the docks. He raced up K Street, dodging passersby and peddlers' carts. The sun roasted his bare head; sweat ran down his face.

Turning the corner onto Second Street, Jem glanced at a tall, ornate tower clock. "Two-forty!" He gasped and ran faster. He wasn't sure what he'd find when he reached the Union Hotel. There was a good chance Aunt Rose would be standing on the threshold, hands on her hips, squinting down the long block. She probably had a scorching speech ready to deliver the minute Jem came into sight.

Half a block from the hotel, Jem slowed his steps. He took a good look at himself in a shop's window and groaned. Sweat plastered his dark hair, and his good Sunday shirt was torn and rumpled from the fight. "I look like one of those riffraff from the waterfront," he said, slumping against the glass. "No one will let me inside the hotel."

He glanced up the street. A horse and carriage was pulling away from the Union Hotel. When it left, Jem spied a lone figure sitting on a bench under the awning. The boy was slouched over, his chin resting in his hands. He didn't move.

"Nathan!" Jem called and ran to meet him.

Nathan looked up at the sound of Jem's voice. Then he jumped up from his seat. "Where's Ellie?" he asked, looking around.

A lead weight dropped into Jem's stomach. "What do you mean 'Where's Ellie?' She's here, with you and Aunt Rose."

"No, she's not. I looked all over the docks for her before I gave up and came here."

"I told her to run back to the hotel! Is she upstairs with Aunt Rose?"

Slowly, Nathan shook his head.

"Then"—Jem swallowed—"where is she?"

CHAPTER 11

Missing

When Nathan didn't answer, Jem grabbed his shoulders. "Are you sure you looked for her good?"

Nathan shoved Jem aside. "Of course I did! I called her and looked everywhere. When I couldn't find her, I figured she'd gone back to the hotel. Only"—he paused—"she's not here either. Do you think she's lost?"

Jem didn't know *what* to think. He felt as if a giant fist was squeezing the air from his lungs. *Oh, God, where is she?* He'd left the waterfront never dreaming Ellie might be there instead of at the hotel. *I left her behind!* "We've got to go back," he said. "We have to find her."

"It won't do any good," Nathan said. "I looked up and down the wharf for two blocks in both directions. She's not there. She either lost her way coming back to the hotel or . . ." His voice trailed off, and he bit his lip.

"Or she didn't make it off the *Duchess*," Jem finished. The thought filled him with dread.

"I'm sorry," Nathan said. "I should have stayed behind and kept looking."

"It's not your fault," Jem told him. "It's *my* fault. I shouldn't have sent her ahead. I shouldn't have left her alone for even a minute." A shudder went through him. Pa trusted Jem to look after Ellie and keep her out of trouble. "What am I going to tell Pa?" he asked weakly.

"You don't have to tell him anything yet," Nathan said. "He hasn't returned from Folsom. But we have to tell Mother." His look turned worried. "She was fit to be tied when I came back late . . . and alone. I put her off, but—"

"My pa's not here?" Hope soared in Jem. He could find Ellie before his father learned she was missing. "Let's head back to the waterfront and—"

"That's not a good idea," Nathan argued. "Mother is already upset. I can't disappear again. We have to tell her."

"Tell me what, Nathan Frederick?"

Jem and Nathan spun around at the same time. Aunt Rose stood under the awning just outside the hotel doors. From one hand hung her small handbag. A parasol looped over her other arm. She looked dressed for a leisurely stroll through the shops and marketplaces of Sacramento.

Her eyes told a different story. They were darker than Pa's, and when Aunt Rose was angry, they flashed daggers. Usually at the wrongdoer. She had spoken to Nathan, but those dagger eyes were aimed at Jem. They demanded an answer, and somebody better be quick about giving it.

Jem licked his dry lips to stall for time and to think up a good reply. Then he sighed inwardly. There was nothing to be gained by skirting around the truth, not even if something did pop into his head. *Lie not one to another* was too firmly lodged in his heart. Pa was willing to overlook a number of his children's misdeeds, but they better not *ever* be dishonest.

The truth, however, made sweat bead on Jem's forehead and tied his tongue in knots.

"Answer me," Aunt Rose demanded.

Jem winced. "Ellie's missing."

Those two little words set Aunt Rose on fire. If she hadn't noticed Ellie's absence before, she certainly did now. She glanced around frantically for her niece. "Heaven preserve us!" she whispered. Then she hustled the boys into the hotel lobby and pointed them toward the settee.

Jem hesitated before sitting down on the rich, red velvet covering. But Auntie's waving hand prompted him to forget his dusty clothes and obey double quick. He sat, and Nathan plopped down beside him.

"What madness is this?" Aunt Rose asked when she'd settled herself into a wingback chair. She clasped her hands in her lap and bored her razor-sharp gaze into her son. "Nathan, did I not clearly instruct you to keep everyone together and out of trouble?"

Nathan ducked his head and managed a slight nod. "Y-yes, Mother."

Jem kept quiet. His turn would come soon enough. A scolding from Aunt Rose was never any fun, and this one would be ten times worse than any he'd experienced back home. Mostly because he was already kicking himself for letting Ellie out of his sight.

Aunt Rose did not mince words. Jem's ears burned by the time she was finished with him. He meekly said, "yes, ma'am" and "no, ma'am" in all the right places and waited for Auntie's anger to cool.

"Now," she finally said, "I want a full accounting of the events. In order. Then we can determine the best course of action for finding Ellianna."

Jem plunged in. He left nothing out and never paused in the retelling, not even when Auntie caught her breath at the mention of Black Boots and his partner. By the time Jem finished his tale—with plenty of interruptions from Nathan—Auntie was plucking a hankie from her bag and dabbing at her eyes.

"I think she's still aboard the *River Duchess*," Jem said dismally. "Black Boots, or Clay, or whatever his name is, probably teamed up with the captain to think of a scheme to get hold of the gold. Why else would he try to chase us down?"

Aunt Rose sniffed her disbelief. "I hardly think that is the case, Jeremiah," she said, dismissing his words with a wave of her hankie. "It seems farfetched. It is more likely that Ellianna is lost somewhere in the city. We know how flighty she can be at times. And I nearly lost my own way today. The city is filled to the brim with fairgoers and gawkers."

Jem wanted to believe Ellie was lost. It was better than what his gut was telling him. But he knew Ellie better than his aunt did. His sister was not shy. If she lost her way, she'd simply ask a passerby for directions to the Union Hotel.

No, something had happened to Ellie, and it had to do with the steamboat . . . and Black Boots. Jem had been there when the highwayman grabbed hold of Ellie for the second time in two days. He remembered the man's words: *"These kids aren't going anywhere."* Yes, Ellie was aboard the *Duchess*. Jem was sure of it. Why wouldn't Auntie at least consider the possibility? *Because it's too horrible to think about,* he answered his own question.

Aunt Rose stood and motioned the boys to join her. "There is nothing to do but go to the police and report Ellianna's disappearance." She blinked back tears. "We must pray they find her before Matthew returns this evening. I don't want to burden him with this distressing news."

She asked Jem and Nathan to bow their heads—right there in the hotel lobby—while she pleaded with the Almighty to look after Ellie and return her safely.

Jem couldn't agree more with his aunt's heartfelt prayer. A wave of panic washed over him at the thought of telling Pa. If his father returned and found Ellie missing—and knew

Black Boots had come anywhere near his family—he'd storm the *River Duchess* with his pistol blazing.

But not before he skinned Jem for losing his sister.

After twenty minutes of searching, Jem decided that policemen in Sacramento were harder to come by than gold on the old Coulter claim. When they finally located a young officer patrolling the streets, he gave directions to a police station several more blocks away. "Don't worry," he said. "Your little girl will turn up sooner or later."

"I shall worry how I please, young man," Aunt Rose said in a huff. "And I prefer my niece is found sooner rather than later." She turned her back on the policeman and stalked off, skirts flying.

By the time they arrived at the station, Aunt Rose had regained her composure. She calmly climbed the stone steps and waited for Nathan to open the door. Straight ahead, a large oak desk took up half the entry. A police officer with bushy sideburns quickly rose and introduced himself as Sergeant Morris. "How may I help you, ma'am?"

Aunt Rose nodded at Jem, and he rushed through his story. When he finished, he burst out, "Please search the steamboat, Sergeant. I'm sure Ellie's been kidnapped."

Sergeant Morris returned to his seat and tugged on his sideburns in thought. A frown creased his forehead for a full minute. "Kidnapping is a serious charge, young man," he finally said. "Captain Belrose is a man of honor—Southerner though he be. He and the *Duchess* have a good, honest reputation up and down this river." He shook his head. "I don't believe your sister is aboard his ship. But I'll assign a dozen officers to comb the city. We'll find her."

He picked up a pen, dipped it in an inkwell, and held it over a sheet of paper. "Can you give me the girl's description?"

Jem paused. What would Pa do if this city policeman told him something that went against his gut? He wouldn't let it go. Not for a second! "It's a waste of time to look for her in the city," Jem said bravely.

Aunt Rose clucked her tongue and frowned. Contradicting grown-ups went against the Coulter rules of conduct.

Jem stood his ground. "Could you at least make a visit to the *River Duchess?* Ask a few questions? Maybe even search it? Those road agents looked mighty determined to get our town's gold." He took a deep breath and said, "My pa is sheriff of Goldtown. He would explore every possibility, even if he didn't agree with it personally."

An awkward silence fell over the group. Jem's heart thudded hard. To throw his father's sheriff job in the policeman's face was a bold, reckless act.

For an instant, the sergeant's face turned dark. Then he laughed, breaking the tension. He stood up, reached over, and ruffled Jem's hair. "You've a spirited tongue, boy, and an active imagination. I suppose being robbed at gunpoint would make any boy's mind think like a dime novel rather than that of a sensible young man."

Aunt Rose pressed her lips together in silent agreement. She often got after Pa for allowing his children to fill their heads with the fanciful exploits found in the latest dime novel.

Jem gave her a pleading look, however, and she turned to the police sergeant. "Humor my nephew, Sergeant. And me, as well. Please call on Captain Belrose."

Sergeant Morris let out a deep breath. "Yes, *ma'am.*" He turned to an officer standing nearby. "Find Mackey, Warren, and Simmons, then meet me down at the wharf. I'm going to have a few words with the captain of the *Duchess.*"

CHAPTER 12

A Frantic Search

It was a long hike back to the river. By the time Jem and the others reached the wharf, the late afternoon sun hung low in the west, spilling its golden rays over the wide waterway. The docks were busier than ever. Jem heard First Mate Peasley shouting at the workers and deckhands to move faster.

"That man is a real slave driver," Jem muttered to Nathan. "The way he's yelling, you'd think the ship was leaving right now instead of in the morning."

Nathan shrugged and didn't answer.

The boys and Aunt Rose fell in behind the police escort as they made their way up the gangplank. At the sight of the uniforms, most of the activity on shore and aboard the *River Duchess* came to a halt. Curious eyes stared at the visitors. The laboring men used the disruption to rest on barrels and wipe away the sweat running down their faces.

Mr. Peasley greeted the sergeant with respect and quickly sent a deckhand to summon the captain. Jem looked around for Henri. His friend was nowhere in sight. Not far away, Jem saw two more square hatches, just like the one he'd peeked into earlier this afternoon. Men were lowering cargo through the dark holes, into the hold below.

Jem's head snapped around when Captain Belrose appeared. He shook Sergeant Morris's hand, tipped his cap to Aunt Rose, and acknowledged the boys with a smile.

But there was no smile in his dark eyes when he said, "I am on a tight schedule, Sergeant. My departure time has been moved up to later this evening. I have no time for interruptions, so please state your business and let me get back to work."

The sergeant shifted uncomfortably and explained—apologetically it seemed to Jem—why they were there. Halfway through the account, the captain interrupted.

"*Oui, oui,* of course you must search," he agreed, "but you will find no missing girls aboard my ship. Search the *Duchess* from bow to stern, and from pilothouse to cargo hold. I have nothing to hide. You may also question the deck passengers." His black brows drew together. "But please respect my cabin passengers and allow them their privacy as they settle in."

"My men and I will be courteous," Sergeant Morris said, "but our search must be thorough."

Captain Belrose folded his arms over his chest and glared at the boys. "Just do it quickly," he told the policemen. "Delays cost money, and I am behind schedule."

The sergeant nodded to the four officers. They split up and disappeared behind the piles of cordwood that were stacked everywhere on deck. Sergeant Morris then turned to the captain. "If you accompany me upstairs, perhaps it will not be such a disruption to your cabin passengers."

Captain Belrose nodded. "Peasley," he ordered, "wait here with our guests until I return."

When his first mate opened his mouth to protest, the captain shook his head. "Patience, Peasley. We always cooperate with the police. You will make up for the delay when they are gone."

"Aye, sir," Peasley snapped, clearly fuming.

Seeing the jumble of freight—barrels, crates, sacks of

grain, wagon wheels, leather goods, and even livestock—along with passengers arriving on board, Jem slumped. How could five policemen find Ellie in this muddle? Would they squeeze through the dark cargo hold below? Would they search every stateroom, washroom, and storeroom? There must be dozens of hidey-holes on the steamboat.

Captain Belrose returned an hour later with Sergeant Morris in tow. The other officers soon joined them. They looked rumpled and weary. Crawling around a large paddle-wheel boat was clearly not their choice of activity on a blistering, late-summer day.

Jem wanted to ask about Henri, but the captain's unfriendly gaze kept him from doing so. Henri's father had seemed so welcoming earlier that day. What had changed? Was Captain Belrose annoyed merely because of the interruption to his schedule, or were the Sacramento policemen unwanted visitors for another, more important, reason?

"Didn't find nothin', Sarge," Officer Warren reported. He wiped his red face with a large bandana. "Hotter than Hades around those boilers."

"What about you, Mackey?" Sergeant Morris asked.

Mackey shrugged. "I talked to dozens of deck passengers and the crew. Nobody has seen a stray, red-haired girl. Sorry, boss."

Jem didn't think he sounded sorry at all. He sounded glad to be done with this task.

"The engineer saw a redheaded girl fly by like a whirlwind some time ago," Officer Simmons put in. "He's sure she left the *Duchess* the same way she and Henri's other friends boarded—near the wheel housing."

Jem's spirits sagged. Engineer Kelly had no reason to lie. If he thought Ellie had jumped ship, then it must be so. But if Ellie was not aboard the steamboat, then where was she? Lost in the city, like Aunt Rose and the sergeant believed?

He barely listened while Sergeant Morris thanked the captain for his cooperation. Then the policeman wished him safe travels and hustled his men, Aunt Rose, and the boys down the gangplank. Jem didn't jump for joy when the sergeant sent his men to the fairgrounds. He knew Ellie was not there.

"She's not lost," Jem said when the police officer left them in front of the Union Hotel. "They can search the fairgrounds for as long as they like, but they won't find her."

"And you are so certain of this, Jeremiah?" Aunt Rose asked with a catch in her voice.

"Yes, ma'am," Jem replied. "More than ever. If she's not aboard the *Duchess*, then one of the bandits caught her on shore and stashed her in a warehouse. There's plenty to choose from." He kicked a piece of cobblestone that had broken loose from the pavement and lay on the boardwalk. It bounced back into the street.

Fresh tears ran down Aunt Rose's cheeks. She swiped at them with her hankie and turned to enter the hotel. "It is unthinkable that men would go to such lengths to hold hostage a young girl, all for a pile of gold."

Jem didn't know what to say. Aunt Rose had lived in Goldtown for six months. She knew what Frenchy had done to Jem for the sake of gold. She'd heard Pa's stories of the gold fever that took men captive. How was this any different?

It wasn't. Stealing gold for a "cause" was no different than stealing it for yourself. Aunt Rose was probably too frightened to think clearly. It hurt less to imagine Ellie was lost than in the grip of the greedy Knights of the Golden Circle.

"Black Boots has her, Auntie," Jem insisted. "Somehow he's going to use her to get the gold. And . . . and . . ." His voice rose. "We *have* to find her!"

Aunt Rose laid a calming hand on Jem's arm. "Evening is upon us, Jeremiah. We have done all we can. The police searched the steamboat and are now at the fairgrounds. There is nothing more to do but wait for Matthew and. . ." She buried her face in her hankie and stumbled into the hotel lobby, sobbing.

Jem watched her go, startled into silence. He glanced at his cousin, who was staring after his mother.

"I need to go to her," Nathan said. "She's awfully upset. You say Uncle Matt's going to get after you, but think how Mother must feel. She's really the one looking out for Ellie. I sure hope she turns up before it gets too dark." He scowled. "And where is that ol' train, anyway?"

Pa had been gone all day. Surely the whistle would blow soon, telling Jem that the train from Folsom had pulled into the depot down by the river. He wanted Pa, and he wanted him *right now*.

But right now, Jem was the man of the family—a position he decided he didn't like as much as he pretended. "Go take care of your mother, Nathan," he said. "I want to sit out here awhile and think."

Nathan nodded and hurried into the hotel.

Alone at last, Jem collapsed onto the bench seat under the Union's awning. The hotel faced west, but tall buildings across the street kept the setting sun out of Jem's eyes. He cupped his chin in his hands, rested his elbows on his knees, and watched the evening traffic roll by.

Regret for not keeping Ellie by his side weighed heavily on him. "I'm sorry, God," he prayed softly. "I made a mess of things today. Where is she?" He heard the long, deep blast from a departing steamboat and added, "Please help me find her."

When Jem opened his eyes, he saw a tall, black youth crossing the busy street. He looked in quite a hurry. Jem held his breath when the boy barely missed being run over by a wagon. Crazy fellow!

The boy stepped up to Jem, panting in his haste. "S'cuse me, suh. This here the Union Hotel?"

Jem nodded. "That's right."

The youth relaxed. "I's lookin' for a sheriff named Coulter. Kin you ask at the desk what room he's in?"

Jem stood up and faced the older boy. "What for? Why do you want to see him?"

"I got this-here note for him." He held up a cream-colored envelope clutched in his hand.

"I'm Jem Coulter. The sheriff is my father. I'll take the note."

The boy stepped back and shook his head. "No, suh. I was told to give it to the sheriff, and that's what I aim to do."

"All right, then," Jem said, frowning. "Come with me. I'll take you to our room."

Pa wasn't there, but he'd be back soon. Maybe the boy could be convinced to leave the message with Aunt Rose. Jem led him into the lobby and up the stairs, deep in thought. Why was somebody sending Pa a note by messenger boy? He was no wharf rat, either. His clothes were clean and pressed. Some rich folks' servant? Wells Fargo? It could be that something had happened to the gold.

"What's your name?" Jem asked at the second landing.

"Silas."

Jem stopped. "Henri's Silas? The cabin boy on the *River Duchess*?"

Silas grinned. "Yes, suh. You know Henri?"

"Yes." Butterflies began to chase each other around in Jem's stomach. "Is the note from Henri?"

"No, suh," Silas said. "Cap'n give it to me, but somebody else wrote it."

"Do you know what it says?" He started up the last flight of stairs.

Silas shook his head. "I can't read, but I know the cap'n's writing, and this ain't it. Don't know whose it is."

Jem didn't ask any more questions; he had a pretty good idea who had written the note. He burst into Aunt Rose's hotel room, where he found her and Nathan sitting on the bed. Nathan had an arm around his mother.

"This is Silas from the *River Duchess*," Jem said. "He's got a note for Pa."

The boy looked around nervously. "Don't see no sheriff."

Aunt Rose stood up and held out a shaky hand. "It's all right, young man. I'm his sister. You can give the note to me."

"I dunno . . ." Silas began, backing up a step.

"If you don't do what she says, I'll rip it right from your hand," Jem said. He clenched his fists and closed in on the dark youth. "Now, *give her the note*."

Silas gulped and handed it over.

"Thank you," Aunt Rose replied and tore open the envelope. "Nathan, find a coin for this young man and show him the door."

"Oh, no, ma'am." Silas didn't move. "I gotta wait for an answer. Can't go back 'til the sheriff tells me 'yes' or 'no.' Sorry, ma'am."

"Yes or no about what?" Jem demanded.

Silas shrugged. "Dunno, suh. Just 'yes' or 'no.'"

Aunt Rose waved everyone into silence while she scanned the creamy paper. Then her face turned white and her hand flew to her mouth. "Tell him 'yes,'" she whispered, just before she crumpled to the ground in a dead faint.

ᵈ CHAPTER 13 ᵉ

An Impossible Demand

Jem gasped and fell to the floor beside his unconscious aunt. What had the note said to make her swoon? He'd never seen her collapse like this before, not even when Ellie brought a garden snake into the kitchen. Aunt Rose had just grabbed a frying pan and promised to whack them both if Ellie and the creature did not clear out "this instant."

Ellie had skedaddled, learning that day who was boss of the kitchen.

"Auntie!" Jem patted her pale cheeks. "What's wrong? Wake up."

Nathan joined him, white-faced. "Mother!"

While his cousin took over trying to revive Aunt Rose, Jem found the note that had fluttered from her fingers when she collapsed. With trembling fingers, he smoothed the paper out and read,

> We have something you want. You have something we want. Bring the goods by land to the head of Steamboat Slough three hours after moonrise and wait there for the boat.

There was no signature and no mention of the gold. Nor did the note identify which steamer would be waiting at Steamboat Slough—wherever *that* was. Pa probably knew. After all, the instructions were meant for him.

To anyone else, the note's message would sound vague, but to Jem it was crystal clear: Ellie was being held aboard the *River Duchess*. He didn't need the unwritten "or else" to know they'd probably never see her again if Pa didn't give those *Snakes* of the Golden Circle the Midas gold.

Clutching the note, Jem shot to his feet with a cry of fury. Just as quickly, he felt light-headed. By now, Aunt Rose had come around and was sitting on the bed with Nathan at her side. Jem fell beside them to catch his breath and think what to do next.

"Kin I go?" Silas asked. He stood by the door, rubbing one bare foot over the other. He looked fidgety at the sight of a fainting lady and a jumpy boy.

"No!" Jem shouted, but Aunt Rose silenced him with a firm hand on his arm.

"Let him go, Jeremiah," she said, strangely unruffled. It appeared that Aunt Rose had fainted, revived, and was now ready to deal with whatever she must. She looked at Silas. "Tell the writer of these grisly demands 'yes.'"

Silas accepted a small tip and bolted from the room.

As soon as the door closed, Jem leaped up and started pacing. He felt close to tears, he was so scared. "Why did you say yes? You know Pa can't give them the gold. It's not his. He can get it out of the safe, but that's the same as stealing."

"Jeremiah, calm yourself," Aunt Rose said. She drew him down beside her and pulled him close.

Jem couldn't sit still. Part of him knew Pa *would* give away the gold. He'd do it to save Ellie. "If he gives them the gold, we can't go back to Goldtown. Not ever. Pa could never pay back eighty-five thousand dollars to Mr. Sterling." He squirmed and rubbed the wetness from his eyes. "We'd be on the run. Probably have to hide out in Mexico for the rest of our lives. Maybe even—"

"Hush," Aunt Rose said, smoothing Jem's sweat-dried hair back in place. "I doubt Matthew will have to give away the gold. But a 'yes' will give him time to come up with a plan. Maybe he can ask the army for help, or the police. Or, it may be as simple as giving them the gold to get Ellianna back safely, then telegraphing San Francisco to board the steamboat when it docks."

"By that time, they'll have hidden the gold in a deep, dark hole," Jem said. "I've been aboard the *Duchess*. It's huge! The police didn't find Ellie; no one will find the gold, either. Or they could land anywhere along the river and move the gold to a wagon." Jem shook his head in despair. "If Pa trades the gold, it will be gone. For good."

"And if he doesn't . . ." Aunt Rose began.

"I know," Jem said. He broke away from Aunt Rose and stood up. "They'll do something horrible to Ellie. Maybe dump her in the river or abandon her in San Francisco. We have to do something!"

Trouble is, you have no idea what that something should be, a little voice taunted. Jem gritted his teeth. He felt caught at the bottom of a deep mining hole, with sides too slippery to claw his way out. Instead of plans filling his head, tears overflowed. He brushed them away. There was no time to feel sorry for himself or Ellie.

Jem could think of only one thing to do. "I'm going to the depot to wait for Pa."

His father would know what to do. He wouldn't even yell at Jem for losing Ellie. Not now. He'd rescue his daughter first then get after Jem all the way back to Goldtown. Jem suddenly couldn't wait for that scolding—just so long as Ellie was sitting there right beside him.

Aunt Rose gave her permission with a quick nod. "Yes, that might be best. Tell him about the note and suggest that he hurry." She smiled at Jem. "The good Lord is watching out for Ellie, no matter where she is. He'll keep her in His hands. Don't fret so, child."

Jem knew he would fret less if he could do more. Until then, he couldn't help worrying.

"Want some company?" Nathan asked.

It was getting late. Jem didn't like the idea of going to the depot in the dark, but he shook his head. "I'll be fine. I know the wharf pretty good by now. You stay here in case more messages come."

Jem was out the door and down the stairs before he could change his mind. He darted into the street, which had come alive now that the sun had set. Jugglers, peddlers, and entertainers of all kinds jammed the sidewalks. Streetlamps burned brightly. Did Sacramento ever sleep? Goldtown didn't seem to. Nighttime back home was often more lively than during the day.

Jem figured it was probably the same in every town and city. He dodged the bystanders and soon found himself along the wharf.

He had to pass by the *River Duchess* on his way to the railhead, a couple blocks away. Torches in iron baskets blazed from tall poles along the levee, lighting up the dock like noonday. Men scurried to finish loading cargo. Passengers swarmed the decks. Overhead, black clouds billowed from the boat's two smokestacks.

Jem quickened his pace. He wanted to find Pa before the ship steamed away.

"Jem!"

He spun around. A shadowy figure was clomping down the gangplank. It made its way through the dock crowd and stopped beside him. Henri was all smiles. "Did you come to wish me *bon voyage?*"

100

Jem didn't waste words answering. He grabbed Henri's shoulders and yelled, "Where's Ellie?"

Henri jumped back, breaking free of Jem's grip. "What are you talking about? How would *I* know where your sister is?"

"She's somewhere aboard the *Duchess*," Jem said.

"How can that be? She ran to safety, *non*? She went to shore before you left my cabin."

Jem shook his head. "Your father is in cahoots with those road agents. They kidnapped Ellie so they can trade her for the gold my pa brought down from the mine."

"Not possible," Henri said, shaking his head. "*Papa* would never—"

"You don't know that!" Jem felt like pounding the boy. He clenched his fists but kept them firmly at his sides. "The police have looked everywhere. They even searched the *Duchess*. Then Silas brought a note to the hotel. No signature, but I know who wrote it. That Clay fellow. It's just the kind of sneaky trick he'd think up to get the gold back, and he's pulled your father right into it."

Henri's face paled. "Silas brought a note?" His gaze darted to the steamboat. "Silas did go on an errand earlier this evening. He returned not long ago and went straight up to the pilothouse."

Jem could not afford to stand around much longer. He stepped away. "I have to find my pa before the steamboat leaves."

Henri caught Jem's sleeve. "Wait. I do not want to believe it, but there might be some truth in what you say. *Papa* is worried. The South . . ." He swallowed, as if the words would not come out. "The South is losing the war. Everything we have is tied up in our steamboats. The *Duchess* is safe here in California. But the others are still in New Orleans. If the Confederacy loses, my family will be ruined."

"What are you saying?" Jem demanded.

"I am saying that *Papa* may be desperate enough to help the South any way he can." Henri looked stricken. "The Knights of the Golden Circle are honorable men. They might try to smuggle gold for the cause, but they would never, *ever* hurt a young girl. This I promise on my life. If she is aboard, I will find her and keep her safe."

Jem didn't answer right away. It was a gallant offer, but Henri was just a boy like himself. Against men such as Black Boots, Henri had no hope of keeping Ellie safe. On the other hand, he seemed to know the *River Duchess* inside and out. Perhaps . . .

Jem listened for the train's whistle but heard nothing. By the time the train from Folsom rolled in, it might be too late to rescue Ellie. A sudden, outrageous idea clicked in his head. "Get me aboard, Henri," he said quickly. "Help me find Ellie. Together, we can get her off the boat."

"Non, non!" Henri backed up a step. "The cargo deck is now so full that we cannot jump aboard like we did this afternoon. The gangplank is the only way on or off. Mr. Peasley and the clerk are both still there, keeping watch over what comes and goes."

"Please!"

"I cannot bring you aboard without you being seen," Henri insisted. "The first mate would catch you, and he does not treat stowaways kindly. And rightly so."

"I'll take the chance," Jem said. "We can run fast. You can hide me."

Henri shook his head. "If what you say is true about the highwaymen, then they are also on board. If you are caught, those ruffians will have two hostages instead of one. Let me find her myself." He paused. "Surely, what I say makes sense!"

It made sense, all right. Trouble was, there was no way Jem was going to let that steamboat leave Sacramento with Ellie on board by herself, alone and scared. Henri didn't count. If Pa wasn't back in time, then it was up to Jem. Maybe he couldn't get her off, but he would find her and stay with her until Pa figured out what to do.

He studied the activity on the wharf. Most of the cargo had been brought aboard. The men were loading the rest of the firewood now, filling every remaining gap on deck. The huge firebox needed cords and cords of wood to heat the boilers, creating steam to turn the paddle wheels.

Seeing the men carrying the three-foot-long logs gave Jem an idea. "Henri, if I can get aboard on my own, will you help me find Ellie?"

Henri followed Jem's gaze and frowned. "What are you thinking?"

"I'm strong, and I haul firewood all the time." He pointed to the men. "I've grown a couple of inches this summer. I'm nearly as tall as some of those smaller fellows. I can pretend I'm—"

"You're out of your mind," Henri cut in. "Your shirt is ripped, but you look nothing like those dirty dock workers and deckhands. You could never blend in."

Jem looked down at his ruined Sunday shirt and knickers. They were city clothes, no matter how torn and filthy. Henri was right. He would never blend in dressed like this. Then he smiled. "Don't worry, Henri. I'll get aboard. Will you hide me when I do?"

Henri gave Jem a halfhearted nod. "*Oui.* If you insist on boarding. But how will you—"

Jem turned and hurried off. "You'll see," he called over his shoulder. "I'll blend in so well that even *you* won't recognize me."

⊰ CHAPTER 14 ⊱

Jem's Daring Plan

Jem left Henri gaping and slipped into the crowd of workers. A minute later he was crouched behind a dwindling stack of cordwood. Nearby, dockworkers pulled logs from the pile and lugged them up the gangplank.

He had to hurry. The *River Duchess* looked packed to the rafters. Seeing the smoke pouring out of the flues, Jem knew the engineer was building up a good head of steam in those tricky boilers. All too soon, the side-wheeler would be heading downriver.

Jem spied his target. The dockworker was a small, lanky fellow, with "lazy" written all over him. He shuffled around the stack of wood, taking twice as long as the others to choose his load and carry it aboard. Best of all, he was wearing an oversized jacket and a scruffy cap.

Perfect. Jem sat back on his heels and waited for the man to return for more wood. While he waited, he felt in his pocket for his gold pouch. A twinge of sadness flickered through his mind, but he slammed it down. "No regrets," he whispered. "Just do it."

Jem pulled out the pouch and squeezed it. He'd worked long and hard for his pile, squatting in the icy spring runoff until he couldn't feel his hands or feet. During the summer months, he'd slopped through the dribbling, muddy creek and sweated for each flake and nugget.

Looking down at his pouch, Jem thought about the knife he had planned to buy this week. There were also all kinds of foods he wanted to taste at the state fair. He even hoped to buy a little pig to raise and sell later this fall as sausage, bacon, and ham.

Jem swallowed the lump that suddenly lodged in his throat. "Don't think about it," he told himself. "I can always pan more gold next spring." Then, before he changed his mind, he opened the pouch. Poking around, he drew out a dozen kernel-sized nuggets and slipped them into his pocket.

He felt a little better for holding something back. *And I still have my big nugget at home.*

The clatter of falling wood brought Jem back to the business at hand. The skinny fellow had returned. He stood close by, cursing the logs and rubbing his leg. A second later, he tripped and let out a stream of words that made Jem gape in wonder. Not even in Goldtown had he heard such salty language.

The man righted himself and reached out to cuff Jem. "Outta my way!"

Jem dodged the blow and quickly stood to face him. Seeing him up close, Jem felt pity. This dockworker wasn't lazy; he was just an old man who looked worn out. It was a mystery why the first mate had hired him to haul cargo in the first place.

Jem cleared his throat. "Mister, will you sell me your coat and cap?"

The man squinted at Jem from under a stained and filthy brim. "You loco? I'd hafta turn around and buy me another. Now, get outta here!" He bent over the stack of wood.

"I'll pay *gold*," Jem said, lifting his pouch.

Like he hoped, the man paused and looked up. "Lemme see."

Jem snorted. "You think I'm a greenhorn? Drop your coat and cap between us. Then I'll show you my pile."

The old man looked interested. He shook off his coat and whipped the cap from his balding head. "I hit color back in '51," he said, tossing the clothes to the ground. "Angel's Camp. Didn't do too bad. But it played out mighty quick." He grinned, revealing a mouth full of rotting teeth.

"I work a claim near Goldtown," Jem said warily. He stood ready to flee if the man tried to steal his gold. Loosening the pouch's strings, he poured a bit of dust and flakes into his hand. "I'll trade my poke for your clothes. You can buy nicer ones, and you won't have to work the docks anymore."

The man leaned forward. His eyes glinted at the sight of Jem's gold. "It's the pure stuff." He scratched his chin. "Why trade?"

"None of your business," Jem said, yanking the pouch closed. "Is it a trade or not?"

The former miner gave Jem a look of grudging respect and kicked the raggedy pile of clothes closer. "Fair enough." When Jem tossed him the pouch, the man took off, disappearing behind a warehouse.

Jem watched him go then bent over the clothes. The rancid smell of stale whiskey mixed with body odor slapped him in the face. He gagged. "Please, God, I can put up with the smell. All I ask for is no lice." But even if the lice of a thousand bodies had taken up residence in these clothes, Jem knew he'd still wear them.

Cringing, he jammed the cap on his head and reached for the jacket. It was stiff with grime. The stench nearly overwhelmed him, but he held his breath and put the coat on. He found two buttons that had not been torn away and fastened the garment over his shirt. As a final touch, Jem scooped up a handful of dirt and rubbed it on his face. Then he lowered the grungy cap brim over his forehead and reached for the cordwood.

Yard-long sections of dry timber weren't heavy, but they were awkward. Jem wrestled three lengths in his arms and headed for the gangplank. He hoped his new stench would keep Mr. Peasley and the clerk from getting too close when he passed them.

He mingled with the dockworkers, falling in place behind two burly black men headed for the gangplank. Before Jem knew it, he was aboard. He passed the first mate and the clerk without being stopped. Apparently, firewood didn't need to be checked off on the ship's manifest.

A stroke of luck at last!

He hurried after the two men, stacking his load where they did, in a nook near the paddle-wheel housing. When they turned to go, Jem ducked behind some barrels marked "nails." He waited a few minutes then cautiously peeked around the cargo. Nobody seemed to notice he'd stayed behind.

Jem felt giddy with relief. *This is a lot easier than I figured.*

By now, the *River Duchess* was not only packed full with tons of cargo but also bursting at the seams with people. They crowded the lower deck wherever there was room. Wealthier passengers traveled in luxury on the upper decks. They were no doubt settling into their staterooms for a long and pleasant night cruise down the river.

The fear of getting caught while boarding had drained Jem of all energy. For a moment he couldn't remember what he should do next. Then it came to him: Henri's cabin. Where was it? Jem closed his eyes and tried to remember. *Two decks up.*

Keeping clear of the passengers, Jem quickly made his way toward the stern stairway. He hoped he could avoid the deckhands too. They would put him to work in an instant.

As he walked, Jem felt a sense of urgency all around him. Men were hastily stowing the last of the stores. *I don't want to ride a steamboat. I want off!* He walked faster. Maybe there was time to find Ellie and get to shore before the *Duchess* left port.

His hand closed around the stair railing just as a sudden, vicious jerk wrenched him backward. "Where do ya think *you're* off to?" a sneering voice demanded. "Get back to the hold and stow the rest o' the cargo, scum." The unseen man tightened his grip on Jem's neck and yanked.

Jem struggled against the choke hold. He couldn't breathe. He couldn't break free. He flopped helplessly as the deckhand dragged him along. Blood rushed to his head and pounded in his ears. Just when he was sure he'd pass out, the man gripping his neck let go and gave him a brutal shove. "Get to work."

The cargo hold lay only four feet below the deck, but it felt a lot lower to Jem. He bounced down the few steps and landed on the rough planks with a groan. Gasping, he drew in sweet air and looked up. A shaggy head was blocking most of the light. "Shake a leg!" the man yelled.

Jem scrambled to his feet. *Clunk!* His head hit the low ceiling. Tears stung his eyes, and he rubbed vigorously through his cap to deaden the pain. Looking around, he saw a long, dark passageway crammed full of crates, barrels, and sacks on either side. Jem strained his eyes to see through the dark. Two pinpoints of light glimmered in the far distance, toward the bow of the ship. A steady stream of thumping and cursing echoed throughout the hold.

"I've got to get out of here," he whispered in horror. At least he could rule out Ellie being kept in this place. It was jam-packed.

Suddenly, the square of light above Jem turned dark. A moment later, a heavy sack of something—probably grain—landed near Jem's feet. He looked around to find a free corner to stow it in. Two more sacks tumbled down before he'd put the first one away.

By the time Jem found places for the sacks that kept raining down on him, he was sure he'd never be able to straighten up again. He'd never worked so hard or fast in his life, dragging a sack and piling it out of the way before another took its place. All the time, he stayed hunched over to avoid smacking his head against the beams.

When no more sacks fell, Jem took a chance. He climbed the steps, poked his head through the hatch, and looked around. The boat's lanterns had been lit, casting dark shadows over the deck. Terrified that he might become trapped inside the hold, Jem scrambled out and crept into the darkness. He paused, trembling all over, and tried to stretch the kinks out of his back.

From everywhere on board, he could hear the sound of people's voices mingling with the braying of donkeys and the

lowing of cattle. Was there anything this steamboat did not carry downriver? He crouched in the shadows, longing to take off the foul-smelling jacket. He felt itchy and hoped it was his own sweat and not a bunch of crawly critters.

Long minutes passed before Jem decided it was safe to move again. He stood up and winced when his back protested. "I've got to find Henri."

Suddenly, the *River Duchess* blew her departing whistle. Jem's hands flew to his ears and his jaw clenched. The noise nearly made him jump out of his skin. On the heels of the deafening blasts, the deck began to vibrate. Nearby, a sloshing and slapping sound came from inside the thirty-foot-high wooden housing. The paddle wheels were turning; the steamboat was on its way.

A minute later, Jem heard the shrill sound of a train whistle. His heart slid into his stomach. Pa was back, but he was too late. Jem and Ellie were trapped, and headed downriver to parts unknown.

CHAPTER 15

Stowaway

Once the *River Duchess* steamed away from the wharf, Jem realized his raggedy disguise might become a problem. The dockworkers had been left on shore, and the deckhands would soon recognize him as an intruder. Mingling with the deck passengers seemed the best way to avoid more trouble. And it offered a chance to rid himself of the stinking clothes.

Jem shed the coat and cap and dropped them over the side with no regrets. Gripping the railing, he watched the pile of rags bob and swirl in the dark current. Then they disappeared out of sight, dragged under by the force of the powerful paddle wheel.

"Most expensive getup I ever bought," Jem said, giving the clothes a wave of good riddance. He'd promised himself that getting aboard was worth the price he paid, but still . . .

He sighed. It *had* been a nice pouch. "It's only gold," he told himself firmly and started to walk away.

The steamboat lurched, picking up speed. Jem's stomach turned over and he clutched the railing again. He'd never ridden on top of the water before. His whole body jiggled from the vibrations of the steam engine. Not far away, the huge boilers were building up pressure. *Very unsafe contraptions.*

Jem swallowed his fear and tightened his hands around the railing to steady himself. Then he pulled his gaze from the dark river and looked toward shore. The burning lights along the wharf were growing smaller and smaller. A full moon rose in the distance.

By now, Pa must be at the depot. Soon, he'd return to the hotel, thinking everything was fine, only to discover that both of his children were missing. Aunt Rose would collapse in another faint, and Nathan would be left to explain. "I'm sorry, Cousin," Jem whispered.

He shook himself free of his gloomy thoughts and stepped away from the railing. Time to get busy and find Ellie. It didn't take long before his feet felt steadier and he could walk without tripping. *This is just a calm river,* he thought. *How did Nathan manage a stormy, six-month sea voyage?*

Jem soon joined the passengers. He seemed to fit right in. No one paid him any attention—not even the officers—until he tried to climb the steps to the next level. "Keep to your own," a voice growled, and a rough hand shoved him back.

Stunned, Jem righted himself. It appeared that the poorer deck passengers were kept away from the wealthier ones traveling on the upper decks. How would he ever reach Henri's cabin? For nearly an hour, Jem lurked near the stairs, waiting for a chance to sneak past the guard. Nothing changed. The stern-faced man was as watchful as a wolf guarding its kill.

Finally, a sudden clattering on the steps above and a familiar voice made Jem want to shout in relief.

"That boy down there," Henri called to the guard. "Tell him to come up here at once. I want him to do something for me."

When the deckhand pointed to Jem, Henri nodded. "Yes, that one. Tell him to hurry."

Jem didn't need to be told. He raced by the guard and

up the steps before the man could relay Henri's orders. Together, the boys ran along the deck, ducking around passengers lounging there. The rest were either in their staterooms or dining in the large, fancy room Jem had seen earlier today—the one with the chandeliers. Henri took Jem the long way around to avoid passing through it.

"I've been looking for you for over an hour," Henri said when he led Jem to an out-of-the-way corner where they could rest and talk. "When you never came to my cabin, I thought you had been caught, or were unable to slip aboard. Then I remembered that even if you did make it, it would be even harder to . . ." His voice trailed off and he wrinkled his nose. "Phew, what is that smell?"

"The jacket I traded for a disguise was pretty ripe," Jem said. "I tossed it overboard, but my shirt hung on to the stink." He shrugged. "I can't really smell it anymore."

"Well, *I* can," Henri said, backing up to keep his distance. Then he went on. "I've been busy looking for Ellie. Your sister is not being kept in the engine room or anyplace else on the cargo deck. I looked there right away."

"She's not in the hold either," Jem said. "It's crammed full."

Henri's eyebrows rose. "You have been in the hold?"

Jem shuddered. "Unfortunately." He explained what had happened and how he'd gotten out. "I've decided I never want to be a deckhand or cargo handler. Not *ever*."

"I don't blame you," Henri agreed. Then he frowned. "That leaves just the two other decks and the pilothouse," he said. "But I found an excuse to go up to the pilothouse, and she's not there."

Jem's heart fluttered with hope. His new friend had indeed been busy. "Thanks, Henri. That narrows it down. Maybe we'll find her soon. Then you can show us a way off this boat before it reaches Steamboat Slough."

Henri's dark eyes turned worried. He chewed on his lip and said, "That will not be easy. There is one stop before the slough. I think it is called Tucker's Landing. If there are no passengers to off-load, *Papa* may skip it and head straight for the slough. The *Duchess* is traveling faster tonight, and *Papa* seems in a hurry. You might be stuck on board for a long time unless, of course, you plan to jump off?"

The fluttering of Jem's heart turned to a dull, heavy thumping. What good was finding Ellie if he couldn't get them both off the steamboat and away from the kidnappers? If they stopped at a landing, he was sure they could make it to shore. But the thought of jumping overboard mid-river made Jem shudder. They would have to depend on river debris—logs and such—to stay afloat. It was a risk he did *not* want to take.

"We'll find Ellie," Henri was saying. "I know this ship like I know my own home. Back in New Orleans, Silas and I played hide-and-seek many times aboard the *Duchess*. He always found the best places to hide." The French boy snapped his fingers. "Why did I not think of this sooner? We should find Silas. That cabin boy usually knows more than he lets on."

"He might know where Ellie is?" Jem asked.

Henri shrugged. "Maybe. But even if he does not, he knows more hiding places aboard this boat than the rats do." He laughed and urged Jem to follow him.

Jem was more than happy for any extra help, but finding Silas was no easy task. Twice they were nearly caught sneaking around. First, Mr. Benz, the clerk, hailed Henri. Jem ducked into a washroom just in time and cowered there until Henri assured him the coast was clear.

A few minutes later, Mr. Peasley came by, breathing fire. The boys heard the first mate from a long ways off. "Biggest, foulest mouth on board," Henri muttered. He shoved Jem around a corner and faced the officer.

"What in blazes are you doing, running around on deck in the dark, boy?" Mr. Peasley shouted. "The *Duchess* hits a snag and *splash!* Over the side you go." He scowled and leaned closer. "I don't fancy fishing you outta the drink, so get to your cabin and stay there."

"Yes, sir."

As soon as the first mate swaggered away, Jem came out from hiding. Henri made a face and kicked at the deck planking. "*Voyou!* I wish *Papa* would fire him and get a new first mate."

Instead of obeying Mr. Peasley's bossy orders, the boys took off in the opposite direction. They finally cornered Silas near the captain's quarters just under the pilothouse. The cabin boy was carrying an armload of soiled laundry.

"Evenin', Mr. Henri," Silas said with a wide grin. "Where you been all day? I—" Then he noticed Jem, and his mouth fell open. "I seen you before. What you doing here?"

"Never mind," Henri said. "We don't have time for your fool questions. First of all, where's *mon père?*"

Silas rolled his eyes toward the ceiling, to indicate the pilothouse. "I fetched him a cup o' coffee and a plate o' doughnuts not more 'n ten minutes ago. It's a right-pretty sight up there, Mr. Henri. The full moon jus' comin' up over the—"

"Hush!" Henri ordered, but he seemed to relax. Knowing Captain Belrose was holed up in the pilothouse made Jem relax too. "Tell me, Silas," Henri went on, "and tell me quick. Have you seen a girl aboard? Not a passenger, but locked up and hidden away somewhere? She's got dark red hair done up in two pigtails."

"She's about so tall," Jem added, lifting his hand to his shoulder. "And she's wearing a blue and yellow calico dress."

Silas's head bobbed up and down. "I sure have, Mr. Henri. Brought her a supper tray earlier. Cap'n told me she's a runaway he's taking back to her folks downriver."

"She's not!" Jem burst out. "She's my sister and—"

"Go on, Silas," Henri cut in, red-faced at his father's lie.

"I don' know nothin' 'bout that, suh," Silas said. "But that lil' miss is full o' fire. And she sure can tell tales! Why, she done told me the biggest whopper I ever did hear, something 'bout kidnappers and gold and . . ." He rolled his eyes and laughed. "I s'pect she need a good lickin' for telling such lies."

"It's Captain Belrose who's lying," Jem said. "Remember that note you brought to the hotel?"

Silas's dark eyes turned worried. He licked his lips and said nothing.

"Answer him," Henri ordered.

Silas managed a weak nod. "Yes, suh. But please don' tell the cap'n I never seen the sheriff. He'd skin—"

"It's a ransom note," Jem interrupted, clenching his fists. He went nose to nose with the older boy. "Do you know what that means, Silas?"

"No, suh. What's ran-som?" He backed up against the captain's door and stared down at Jem.

"It means somebody wants to trade Ellie for a gold shipment Jem's father brought to town yesterday," Henri said. "And somehow, *Papa* is being forced—"

"Enough explaining," Jem broke in. "Take us to Ellie. *Right now.*"

Silas's eyes opened so wide that Jem could see the surrounding whites. "I can't do that, suh," he said, trembling. "I'm taking care of her. Cap'n will skin me alive if I mess with his orders."

"Tell us where she is," Henri said. "I will keep you out of trouble with *mon père.*"

Jem shot Henri a look that read, *How will you do that?*

Henri shrugged, clearly uncertain of anything right now.

Silas licked his lips and gripped his armload of linens tighter. "Well . . . uh . . ." He wrinkled his brow. "Let's see. Ya know that bunch o' staterooms starboard, back by the . . ." He shook his head, clearly trying to collect his thoughts. "I mean the ones next to—"

"Just *show* us!" Jem cut in. Silas seemed frazzled and unable to give simple directions.

"Yes, suh." Without another word, the cabin boy moved off. Jem and Henri followed him as he ducked into a corridor then crossed from one side of the steamboat to the other. He came out on the opposite deck and passed a dozen cabin doors. Very few passengers were quartered on this deck, and they met no one.

Silas stopped and nodded to a door near the back. "In there."

Jem turned the knob and shoved. Nothing happened. He pounded on the door. "El—"

Henri clapped a hand over Jem's mouth and yanked him away. "*Shhh!* Do you want to alert the entire deck?" He removed his hand and turned to Silas. "It's locked."

Silas nodded. "Cap'n don't want the lil' miss running off. She might fall overboard and get drownded."

"Do you have the key?"

Silas ducked his head and stared at his armload of soiled linens. "Yes, suh."

Henri lifted his palm. "Well, hand it over."

Clearly frightened, Silas hesitated and looked at the captain's son with pleading eyes. Henri thrust his hand closer. Silas sighed, shifted the laundry to one arm, and dug in his pocket for the precious key.

In a heartbeat, Henri turned the key then stepped away without opening the door. "Jem," he said suddenly. His hands shook. "Before you go inside, I have something to tell you. It will not be easy, and I hope you will not be angry with me."

Jem's mouth went dry. *Open the door!* he wanted to shout. Instead, he swallowed and asked softly, "What is it?"

Henri sucked in a deep breath. "I am sorry, but I have helped you as much as I can. Now, you will have to free your sister and leave the *Duchess* on your own."

Jem's heart raced in protest. "But—"

"No, Jem," Henri said. "I don't know what's going on, but if *Papa* gave the order to lock Ellie up, it must be because those highwaymen made him."

Jem doubted that. The Knights of the Golden Circle were most likely of one mind with their plans to steal the Union gold. But looking at Henri, Jem couldn't say it out loud. His friend looked torn apart.

"I dare not cross him," Henri said. "And besides, I cannot be disloyal. He is *mon père*. I . . . I love him."

There was nothing Jem could say to that. Wouldn't he stand with Pa, even if it didn't feel right at the time? Only a few months before, Jem was sure that Pa taking on the sheriff's job was not right. Jem had been proved wrong and learned that his father knew exactly what he was doing.

Maybe Henri's father knew what he was doing too. *Not likely!* But Jem kept his mouth shut. He didn't want to add to Henri's distress. "You've already helped me plenty," he said, forcing a cheerfulness he did not feel. *"Merci."*

Henri smiled at Jem's attempt to thank him in French. *"Au revoir,* and I'm sorry," he said in farewell. He turned and dashed away, his hand sliding along the railing to keep from going over.

Jem didn't waste another moment. He didn't care if Silas stayed or went. He gripped the knob and gave it a turn. Then he opened the door.

⫷ CHAPTER 16 ⫸

Hide and Seek

A blur of blue and yellow flew at Jem as he crossed the threshold into the tiny cabin. "No, Ellie!" He jumped back, but he was not quick enough.

Armed with a short, wooden rod, his sister swung at Jem, grazing his shoulder. Then her red-rimmed eyes grew huge and she dropped the weapon. It fell to the floor with a *clunk*. "I'm sorry, I'm sorry," she said, collapsing next to the dowel rod. Huge sobs tore from her throat. "I thought you were . . ." Her voice trailed off into more crying.

Jem knelt beside her. His shoulder stung, but it was nothing compared to the tumble he'd taken earlier when he dropped from the rooftop. "Take it easy, Ellie. I'm fine. I'm here. I'll get you out of this fix. Just see if I don't."

"I . . . want . . . Pa," Ellie blubbered. But she let Jem help her to her feet and lead her to the tiny bunk. "Where is he?"

Jem sat down on the bed and pulled Ellie close. "Pa's not here, but I heard the train whistle. He's in Sacramento with Nathan and Aunt Rose by now. Don't worry. I'm sure he's on his way."

Ellie cried harder. "With the *gold!* Oh, he can't give away the gold, Jem. He *can't!*"

But Jem knew Pa would. He had said as much back on the stagecoach, if the highwaymen had not been fooled. *"No gold—not even for the sake of the Union—is worth putting my family and the other passengers in danger."*

"How did you know they want to trade you for the gold?" Jem asked. A slight shuffling near the open door told him that Silas had not moved off. Instead, he came in and shut the door softly behind him. *Good! He's getting an earful.*

"That *beast*, Marcus, said so," Ellie said. Sniffing, she told her tale. "I was almost free, Jem. Almost! I shoulda just jumped in the water and got wet, but I was scared. I kept looking at how far it was from the deck to the levee and then . . ." She paused.

"Then what?" Jem urged. He took her hand and squeezed it. They didn't have a lot of time, but he knew Ellie had to tell him. Once she let it all out, she'd quickly return to being her cheerful, carefree self.

"Somebody grabbed me from behind," Ellie said, gulping back a sob. "I tried to get loose. I wiggled and kicked. He put his hand over my mouth, and I bit it so hard he yelped. But he didn't let go. He just slapped me and hauled me up here. Then he locked me in and left."

Poor Ellie! "What happened then?"

"Nothin' good," Ellie said. "I screamed and pounded on the door and tried to kick out the window so I could escape."

Jem smiled. He could see his sister tearing around the room trying to free herself, just like a wildcat in a sack.

"That Marcus fellow came right back," Ellie said. "He slammed through the door and grabbed me. Then he shook me and said if I didn't shut up he'd gag me and tie me up. So I got real quiet." She let out a shaky breath. "I didn't want to be tied up."

"You did the right thing," Jem assured her.

Ellie kept crying. "He told me not to worry. I wouldn't be

here for long, on account of my daddy would pay plenty to free me. And he would pay in gold." She gulped. "Oh, Jem! I knew what he meant. Then he laughed and locked me up again. I worked like crazy to pull the towel rack down so I'd have a weapon the next time he opened that door."

Ellie's nose was running freely now, and tears splashed down her cheeks. For once, Jem was without a bandana or handkerchief of any kind. He couldn't even offer his shirt. The lingering stink clung to it.

Just as Ellie lifted her skirt to wipe her face, Silas stepped over and dropped a large, white square of cloth in her lap. "Here, missy," he said softly. "And . . . and I's awful sorry I didn't believe you."

Jem and Ellie looked up. Hanging over them, shame-faced, the cabin boy had tears in his eyes. "It looks like y'all are trapped the same as me."

"Does that mean you'll keep quiet about this?" Jem asked. He noticed the key was jammed in the hole on *this* side of the door. They were safe, at least for now. But they couldn't stay here forever. Ellie's kidnappers might show up any minute.

Silas nodded. "Yes, suh." He kicked aside the pile of linens he'd been lugging around and sat down on the floor.

Ellie pointed at Silas. "After Marcus left, *he* came in with a tray of food. I tried to tell him I was kidnapped. I asked him to help me, but he wouldn't. He said I was a runaway and—"

"I'll help y'all *now*," Silas said, giving them a long, sorrowful look.

"Can you get us off the ship?" Jem asked.

Silas grinned. "Sure. I'll take y'all to the very back of the boat. Just hop over the rail and *splash*, you're free." Then he sobered. "That is, if y'all kin swim."

Jem and Ellie looked at each other, then Jem shook his head. "We never needed to learn. There's nothing bigger than

121

a gold-panning creek back home." He stood up and started to pace the tiny stateroom. "What about this Steamboat Slough? Is it a landing?"

Silas frowned. "No, suh. It's where the river splits. The slough is the fastest route to the city. Though"—he scratched at his tight, dark curls in thought—"there's a spot right near the head of the slough, where a boat kin pull close to shore. A landing of sorts. But who'd want to? The bushes and trees is thick as a jungle along there."

Jem didn't tell Silas that it sounded like a perfect, out-of-the-way spot to conduct some sneaky business. Stop the *Duchess*, send a dinghy to shore, and make a quiet trade. "No wonder we're steaming downriver so fast," he said under his breath. "They have to make up for the stop."

No one said anything for the next few minutes. Jem kept pacing and thinking. How much time did they really have? It was way past sundown now, and getting later. Where was Pa? What was he doing? Had he loaded the gold and rushed off to meet the Knights? *What do I do now, God?*

Just then, Silas stood up and stretched. "I hafta get back before the cap'n misses me. You two kin stay here, or I kin show y'all a good place to hide. I could maybe slip y'all off at Tucker's Landing. Water's not deep there. You'll get wet, but that's all."

Jem stopped pacing.

"I know the best hidey-holes on board," Silas continued. "I seen the cap'n stash things he don't want the crew to know about. It's small, but you two kin fit." He turned the key and quietly opened the door. "Follow me."

It was a risk, Jem knew. If Black Boots, his partners, or even the sharp-eyed first mate caught them, they would be trussed up tighter than calves for branding. But staying here was just as risky. Jem pulled Ellie up next to him and nodded at Silas. "Lead the way."

After closing and locking the cabin door, Silas, Jem, and Ellie slipped through the shadows and out on deck. Silas led them around the back of the officer cabins then down another deserted corridor. Jem chuckled softly. *This is too easy!* By now, he felt he knew the ship nearly as well as Henri or any crew member. He'd seen it all—from cargo hold to pilothouse—and ducking into dark corners to avoid suspicious eyes had become second nature.

When Silas cracked open the door to an out-of-the-way storage closet, Jem knew right where he was. "It looks just like the one I hid in already today," he joked, brushing past a mop and pail.

Silas put a finger to his lips, and Jem shut up. Clear at the back, the cabin boy pushed aside a small crate labeled "soap" and slid his hands along the wall. Fascinated, Jem squatted and watched as Silas found a crack and slipped his fingers into it. Bunching his muscles, he took a deep breath and yanked. A piece of the wall moved aside.

Jem's mouth fell open, and he frowned. Did Silas expect Ellie and him to squeeze into that small, black hole? Ellie's grip on his arm told him she didn't think much of the hiding place either. "Do we have to?" she whispered in his ear.

"It's bigger than it looks," Silas said, scooting back from the opening. "Soon as we make Tucker's Landing, I'll let y'all out and drop ya in the river. Ain't far to the dock, so y'all won't drown."

Jem crawled forward and peeked into the cubbyhole. He couldn't see much. The only light spilling into the storeroom came from the narrow corridor outside. He took a deep breath and made his way forward.

"Ouch!"

"What's wrong?" Ellie asked.

"I banged into something. Something heavy." He pushed against a large, rectangular box. It didn't budge. "There's no room for Ellie and me." He backed out. "A couple of boxes are taking up the floor space."

"Lemme see," Ellie said, blocking the hole.

Jem pulled her back. "You'll just get banged up. Let me look around." His eyes were adjusting to the gloomy storeroom, and he peered carefully at the two dark, shadowy objects. A latch and padlock glinted in the half light. The metal corners gleamed too. A strongbox! His gaze flicked to the other container. It was identical. *Two* strongboxes!

Bewilderment, disbelief, then sudden understanding threw Jem's stomach into somersaults. He scrambled backward, away from the hiding place, and crashed against the pail and mop. It tipped over, clattering to the floor. Jem ignored it. "We can't stay here," he whispered. "Not now. Not ever."

"Why not?" Ellie demanded.

Jem nodded at the opening. "I think those two strongboxes are full of gold. They're heavy enough." He took a deep breath to gather his wits. "And I betcha it's *stolen* gold."

⊰ CHAPTER 17 ⊱

Disaster!

Silas fell to his knees and peered into the hidey-hole. He shuddered then quickly slid the panel across the opening. "I's sorry. I thought it was empty."

"Black Boots probably hoped to add the Midas gold to this stash for the South," Jem said. "Can you find us another place to stay out of sight? This one's no good."

All three rose in the gloomy storeroom. Silas crossed his arms and stared off into a corner, deep in thought. When he spoke, he didn't sound too confident. "Might be a washroom outta the way down on the boiler deck." He sighed. "Can't think of nothin' better right now."

Jem and Ellie followed Silas back out on deck and down the staircase to the deck below. Jem paused, gripped the railing, and held his breath at the sight. Across the river, pinpoints of light twinkled through the trees, revealing small villages and a few houses along the banks. A full moon lit up a path in the dark water. The slapping of the paddle wheels sounded friendly. Even the vibrating deck no longer alarmed him.

Close by, the sound of laughter and music floated from the lounge. Passengers were clearly enjoying themselves—playing cards, socializing, and dining. A door opened then closed, and the tantalizing odor of roast pork drifted over Jem. His belly grumbled. *I wish I—*

"Hurry, suh," Silas warned from a few yards away.

Jem took one last look upriver. To his surprise, a large steamboat was trailing not far behind, her decks lit up with torches. She seemed to be in the same hurry as the *Duchess*. Was Tucker's Landing that important of a stop? What was the all-fired hurry in getting there first?

He opened his mouth to ask the knowledgeable cabin boy, when a startled shout went up from the deck above. Angry, pounding feet clomped just over their heads, drowning out the pleasant sounds from the lounge.

Silas ran back to Jem, panting. "*Hurry!* They done figured out your sister's gone!"

Jem leaped into action. He snatched Ellie's hand and tugged her along behind Silas.

"There she is!"

"Where'd the boy come from?"

"Who cares? Go after them!"

Jem looked up. Hanging over the upper deck railing, Clay and Marcus, along with two others, were gaping at the runaways, clearly astonished. The staircase wasn't far away. In no time, the road agents would catch up and overpower them.

Jem wracked his brain to think of a way to delay them. "You better go check your precious gold shipment!" he shouted. "Make sure it's still there."

The men froze. Then Clay swore and turned away. Jem hoped they would rush off to their hidey-hole before realizing that he could no more move those strongboxes than he could move the moon. But their greed and uncertainty might give him and Ellie time.

When he turned to look at Silas, the cabin boy was

shaking in terror. "They seen me," he whispered. "They know I's helping you. My life ain't gonna be worth a—"

What Silas's life was not worth, Jem never found out. Suddenly, an explosion louder than a whole battery of cannon fire shattered the quiet evening. At the same time, a shock wave passed through the steamboat with a force that seemed to separate plank from timber.

The blast threw Jem against the paddle-wheel housing, dragging Ellie with him. Fragments of the ship were hurled in all directions. People screamed. Jem cowered next to the housing. Surely, the steamboat was being blown to pieces! He held Ellie and watched as terrified, confused passengers ran back and forth on deck, wailing and crying for help.

Then the *Duchess* shuddered and listed sharply to one side. Ellie was torn from Jem's arms. She flew against the deck railing, bounced over it, and with arms flailing fell into the dark river below.

Jem was one splash behind her.

Water was everywhere—in his mouth, his eyes, his nose. And it was so *cold!* The warm September evening had made Jem forget how icy creeks and rivers could be, even in the summertime. He wanted to cough, to sneeze, and to scramble out of this watery deathtrap, but he didn't know how. He only knew enough to hold his breath as he felt himself bobbing up, up, up . . .

When his head broke the surface of the water, Jem pulled in one warm, sweet breath. No sooner had he gulped in the air when he found himself underwater once more. Chilly darkness engulfed him; the pale moonlight barely lit up the first few inches of the murky river.

I'm going to drown! The thought paralyzed Jem, scaring him more than anything in his whole life. Not even when he was trapped in the mine earlier this summer had he panicked. He'd been frightened, of course, but he knew as long as they had air to breathe, Pa and the others would eventually dig them out. They only needed to stay calm and wait.

Not now. There was no air here, and nothing to grab on to. Staying calm and waiting meant a quick death in the Sacramento River—especially since he couldn't swim.

And what about Ellie? The horror of letting his sister drown drove Jem's arms and legs into a churning frenzy. He broke the surface and drew in another breath. But he didn't know how to stay on top of the water, and his heavy shoes were pulling him down. *Help me, Jesus!*

Clunk! Something banged into Jem's head. He reached out and felt a piece of debris from the steamboat. In the dark, he couldn't make out what it was, but he didn't care. It was floating, and it didn't sink when Jem wrapped his arms around its sides. He laid his head down against the flat wooden piece and sobbed his thanks to God. *I'm not going to drown. At least, not right away.*

The emergency over, Jem's senses took in his injuries. What he thought was water dripping down his face was actually warm, salty-tasting blood. His nose felt broken, and now that he could breathe again, it hurt—a lot. So did his chest. No doubt he'd cracked a rib when he'd been thrown around on deck.

He took a shallow, painful breath and tried to call Ellie's name. It came out a mere whisper. Jem looked about and saw floating cargo, shivering people clinging to steamboat parts, and terrified animals swimming for shore. But no Ellie.

In the distance, the *River Duchess* drifted helplessly, her bow totally turned around and pointing upriver. The ghostly light of the moon showed Jem where a huge section of the steamboat had blown out. *"Boilers are tricky things,"* the engineer had said. Jem briefly wondered if the man was still alive.

Had scalding water and steam burned him before he could escape?

Jem's thoughts turned to Henri and Silas, and he closed his eyes. Had his friends escaped the blast? Were they aboard, safe? Had they been thrown into the river? Were they . . . were they *dead*?

Jem splashed a handful of water against his face to wash the blood away. "Ellie!" he called again, but he heard no response over the heart-wrenching sounds of moaning and wailing. Jem felt like crying too. He hurt everywhere, but mostly inside. "I couldn't save her," he said, eyes stinging. "I'm sorry, Pa."

Then a heavy hand came down on his shoulder. "You all right?"

Silas's voice sounded prettier than singing angels. "Silas!" Then in the moonlight, he saw Ellie. She was bobbing up and down in the water nearby, facedown on a cabin door, unmoving. *"No!"* He felt sick.

"I fished her outta the river," Silas explained at Jem's stricken look. "She's alive, but mighty quiet. I reckon she swooned."

"Ellie?" Jem paddled closer and touched her on the shoulder. "You awake?"

Ellie lifted her head and stared at Jem without speaking. She looked dazed. A long gash cut across her forehead, where she must have collided with the deck railing before going overboard. One arm looked twisted out of shape. Most likely broken. She licked her lips and said, "I hurt."

"You just lie quiet, and—" Jem winced as he took a breath—"we'll paddle to shore and get you out of the river."

Ellie didn't answer. She laid her head down and closed her eyes.

Jem looked at the Sacramento side of the river. It was a long way off, but he didn't want to keep floating downriver.

Near the middle of the current, the steamboat that had been following the *Duchess* was lit up even more now. Men were lowering longboats into the water.

Jem didn't want to wait for rescue. He wanted out of this river, and soon. "Can you help us get ashore?" he asked Silas.

The cabin boy was clutching a long, wooden plank. He didn't seem any worse for wear, and he looked at home in the water. "Yes, suh. It ain't as far as it looks." Then he sighed, long and deep. "I ain't sure what I'm gonna do," he confessed. "If I go back, Cap'n will learn how I let y'all go. But I been too scared to run off. Heard too many stories 'bout slave catchers."

Jem shook his head, even though the movement made him wince. "Not in California. You can escape and be free here. Besides, the captain probably thinks you're dead."

Silas's mouth widened into a smile. "The good Lord knows that's true enough," he agreed. "There be plenty of dead folks to count before this night is done." His smile faded and his gaze flicked to the wounded steamboat drifting less than a hundred yards away.

Jem shivered, but not from the cold water. Looking at the steamer, his mind felt fuzzy. Everything had happened so fast, and he knew the horror of the accident would not end soon. He watched a lifeboat from the *Duchess* slap into the water. Then another. Wailing passengers and bellowing livestock— all that survived—were clamoring to be freed from the listing steamboat. Who knew if or when it might sink? A few shadowy figures leaped from the decks to take their chances in the river before something worse happened.

A sudden, violent thrashing from behind Jem made him spin around. One of the surviving mules was frantically trying to make its way to shore. Fully harnessed, the poor beast dragged its lead line along, attached to a broken length of railing.

"Come on," Silas said, motioning Jem to his side.

Jem was more than happy to let the older, river-experienced cabin boy take the lead. His mind whirled. He couldn't seem to focus or make decisions. Now that Ellie was safe, all he wanted to do was sleep.

Jem couldn't sleep, though. He had to stay with Ellie. So he mustered enough strength to kick his feet and follow Silas as the youth pulled Ellie's raft toward shore. Jem's eyelids fluttered. It took all his will to keep breathing without making his ribs scream.

"I heard tell 'bout plenty of steamboat mishaps," Silas was saying.

"What?" Jem strained to keep up and listen. It helped him stay awake.

"Boilers explode a lot," Silas said. "Either that, or a paddleboat plows into a snag and *crack!* Down she goes. I seen steamboats go down. One sank so fast they never saved nothin' but the passengers. They was screamin' and yellin', and just one boat to ferry 'em all to shore." He shook his head. "Ten minutes, and she was *gone,* just like that."

Jem peeked back at the battered steamboat. Poor Henri! His folks' livelihood blown up in an instant. What would they do now? If they were still alive, that is.

His face must have showed his sorrow, because Silas said, "Don't you worry none 'bout Henri and the *Duchess.* She won't sink. I s'pect the damage ain't as bad as it looks, but it'll cost a pretty penny to fix her." He paddled faster. "Cap'n will be too busy with repairs to worry 'bout what happens to me."

By the time the riverbank came within spitting distance, Jem felt light-headed. Pain wracked every bone in his body, and he was dog-tired. *Only a few more yards to go,* he kept telling himself, but he couldn't seem to get any closer. Trees and shrubbery slid by like dark sentinels guarding the Promised Land. *You can't come ashore!* they seemed to mock.

Jem reached out to grab a branch, but it slipped through his cold, stiff fingers. The current slapped against his raft. *I can't do this anymore.* His hand flopped to his side, and his feet went limp.

Then everything turned dark.

CHAPTER 18

Delivered

Mr. Jem, wake up. This ain't no place to sleep."

Silas's insistent voice roused Jem from where he lay, sprawled on the bank of the Sacramento River. A few feet away, water splashed at his feet, but the mud against his cheek convinced Jem that he was really and truly on land. He dug his fingers into the soft muck and pushed himself up. Nothing in the whole world felt as good as this wet, sticky dirt!

"Now I know why sailors kiss the ground when they finally reach land after a storm," he said, grinning weakly. "How long was I out?" He glanced around for Ellie and saw her curled up, asleep under some overhanging branches.

"A few minutes," Silas said. "You nearly got away from me. I yanked you off the planking and dragged you ashore."

"Thanks, Silas. You're a real friend. If there's anything I can do to help you get away to freedom, I'll do it."

Silas grinned. He smiled a lot, Jem noticed, even though he looked like a drowned, muddy rat. "I s'pect I'll be fine," the cabin boy said. Then he pointed at the *River Duchess* half-way across the water. The steamboat was no longer drifting. It seemed to be held fast in one place. "Looks like the *Yosemite* tied up to her. Might even tow her back come daylight."

"How do you know the other steamboat's name?" Jem asked, trying to stand. He really needed to find help—and Pa. But pain like a knife shot through his chest, and he carefully returned to the ground. *Maybe I'll just sit still for a bit.*

"I know 'em all," Silas said. "I love the river. I love steamboats. I—" He broke off and sighed. "I sure gonna miss 'em."

Jem followed Silas's hungry-looking gaze and saw how torn the older boy was on the inside. Should he go back to slavery to stay aboard the *Duchess,* and hope Captain Belrose would forgive his disloyalty? Or should he make a break for freedom and become his own man?

Jem knew nothing about slavery personally, but everything Miss Cheney told the class about it made him hope Silas would want to start a new life.

"Listen, Silas," he said, carefully choosing his words. "There's no reason you can't work the river again some day. Hide out here in California 'til the war's over. Then you could hire on as a deckhand in Sacramento aboard another steamboat, or even go back to the Mississippi if you miss it."

Silas pulled on his lip and frowned in thought, but he said nothing.

"Who knows," Jem went on. "You might work your way up to engineer, or maybe even captain."

"Aw, get away with you, Mr. Jem," Silas said, laughing. But his eyes gleamed.

Jem would have laughed too, but he knew better than to let his ribs jab him in pain. Instead, he wondered what they should do now. He wanted Pa, but he had no idea where his father was. *I don't even know where I am,* he thought. Jem hurt too much to work his way through the heavy vegetation to find help, especially with Ellie in tow.

"I reckon we'll sit tight and wait to be rescued," Jem decided wearily. The warm September night made his decision easy. Now that he was out of the chilly water, he was no longer shivering.

Up and down the river, longboats fished folks out of the water. Not far away, a small, steam-powered dinghy was chugging toward shore. Jem heard its engine before he saw the single smokestack and the four men inside.

Silas gasped and ducked behind some brush. "Look, Mr. Jem," he whispered. "See how low that lil' boat's riding? And see who's in it? That Marcus fella. He locked up your sister."

Silas's night vision was better than Jem's. Even with a full moon overhead, Jem couldn't make out their faces. But he believed Silas. "Betcha they're sneaking away with the hidden gold we found on board. Those dirty, rotten thieves."

Jem clenched his fists in helpless anger and watched the small craft hug the shoreline and work its way upstream, back toward Sacramento. Anywhere along the wild, brush-choked riverbank, the men could hide the gold and come back for it later, when the hubbub died down.

That gold belongs to the Union! he shouted silently. It had probably been taken from some other unlucky stagecoach in gold country.

Then Jem let his fists go limp. There was nothing he could do about it. "At least they didn't get the Midas gold," he said, consoling himself. "And Ellie is safe."

"Amen," Silas whispered. "That's most important."

A few minutes later, another boat rowed close, this one loaded with crewmen and frightened, weary survivors. "Yoo-hoo! You on the shore!" a man called. He held up a glowing torch and waved it back and forth. "Want a ride to Tucker's Landing? It's a long walk otherwise."

Jem's heart leaped at the offer. "Yes, sir!" His chest exploded in pain, but he wanted to make sure the officer heard him. "My sister is injured. Can you help her aboard?"

In answer, the boat drew closer. Jem tried to stand and was grateful when Silas gave him a hand. "G'bye, Jem," the former cabin boy whispered in his ear. "I gotta go. I'll find me that mule that came ashore and make my own way."

Jem nodded, pleased. Silas had left off the "Mr." The former slave had made his decision to be free.

In a rush of gratitude for Silas's help, Jem dug into his pocket for the gold he'd kept back earlier that evening. Thankfully, the small chunks were still there. "I knew there was a reason I held on to these." He picked up Silas's hand and dropped the yellow nuggets in his palm. "It isn't much, but it should give you a start."

Silas's eyes grew huge. "It's . . . it's . . . *gold!*"

Jem grinned. "Sure it is. Go with God, Silas. Come to Goldtown if you get the chance. My pa would want to thank you for what you did for Ellie and me."

Silas nodded, then vanished into the woods like a shadow just as the longboat scraped the shore.

"You all right, boy?" the officer asked, stepping up behind Jem. "I'm Turner, first mate on the *Yosemite.*"

"I'll live," Jem said, swallowing the lump that clogged his throat. He would probably never see Silas again. "But my sister's hurt pretty bad."

"We'll take good care of her," Mr. Turner promised. He lifted Ellie gently in his arms and carried her to the longboat.

Ellie whimpered and called out for Pa, but Jem hushed her. "He'll take us to Pa, Ellie. Just go back to sleep and don't give Mr. Turner any trouble."

The boat was crowded, but even in their misery, the *Duchess*'s survivors made room for Jem and Ellie. An older woman with multiple burns on her face and hands cradled

Ellie in her arms. In spite of her obvious agony, she made room for Jem and kindly asked, "What's your name?"

"Jem Coulter. And that's my sister, Ellie."

First Mate Turner's eyebrows rose. "Coulter, you say?" When Jem nodded, he said, "The *Yosemite* was hoping to overtake the *Duchess* at the Landing. We're carrying a small complement of soldiers. We planned to board her and recover the daughter of a small-town sheriff by the name of Coulter."

"That's my pa," Jem said eagerly. All weariness fled. He forced himself to sit up straight. "Where is he?"

The longboat slipped into the water, and two crewmen manned the double sets of oars. "Don't rightly know," Mr. Turner said. "I think he stayed ashore in order to take a wagon at least as far as Tucker's Landing. Don't know what he planned to do with it, though." He smiled. "The lieutenant knows. I'm just the first mate."

Jem pointed upriver, in the opposite direction of the Landing. "There's a little steam dinghy heading that way with a load of stolen gold. Betcha the lieutenant would like to hear about it."

"I bet he would too," Mr. Tucker agreed. "I'll drop you folks at the Landing then head back to the *Yosemite* as quick as I can."

When the longboat pulled up to Tucker's Landing twenty minutes later, Jem strained to see through the crowd. Gawkers, rescuers, and a hoard of survivors crammed the wharf. Torches blazed, turning the landing from nighttime to noonday. Suddenly, a tall figure broke through the mob and stood on the very edge of the wharf. His eyes anxiously scanned the newest arrivals.

"Pa!" Jem cried out, though it made him wince and clutch his chest. He didn't care. He stood up and waved, ignoring his cracked ribs. Pa was waiting. He'd make everything all right.

Pa kept Jem and Ellie overnight in the tiny village of Clarksburgh, the closest settlement to Tucker's Landing. The whole town had turned out to lend a hand to the steamboat's casualties. Churches, the schoolhouse, and private homes overflowed with the injured. Doctors and nurses from as far away as Sacramento rushed to their aid.

Jem soon found himself wrapped up tighter than a mummy.

"To keep your ribs in place while they heal," the kindly doctor explained.

"I . . . can't . . . move," Jem said. He struggled to get comfortable on the narrow sofa in someone's parlor.

"You're not supposed to move," Pa said, sitting down beside him. He picked up one of Jem's hands and squeezed it. "You had yourself quite a day, Son. You've earned the rest. Enjoy it, and thank God He spared your life, and Ellie's." His dark-blue eyes turned sad. "Many aboard the *Duchess* were not so fortunate."

Jem shuddered. He *was* grateful. His broken nose, cracked ribs, and Ellie's broken arm were minor injuries compared to the folks who had been scalded when the boiler ruptured. Others around him lay unconscious with serious head wounds. Still others found themselves with crushed or lost limbs. And the missing or dead? It would be several days before anyone learned the final results of the explosion.

"I reckon I won't be seeing the fair," Jem said, overcome with drowsiness all of a sudden. The doctor must have slipped some laudanum into the potion he'd poured down Jem's throat a few minutes before.

Pa's hearty laugh rang out, making Jem feel warm all over. He reached out and ruffled Jem's hair—gently—and said, "We'll see how you and Ellie feel later this week, after we get back to the hotel."

"I feel fine, Pa," Ellie insisted from her spot on a pile of quilts nearby. "Good as new." She raised her splinted arm two inches. "This arm won't cause me any more trouble. *Please* can we go to the fair?"

Ellie was still begging to see the fair a week later. Jem walked carefully around their hotel rooms to show Pa and Aunt Rose that he felt "nearly new."

Aunt Rose was not convinced. She hovered over her niece and nephew as if they were recovering from the plague. Tears had gushed when Jem and Ellie told their stories. She blamed herself over and over again for not accompanying them to the riverfront that first day. "If only I'd—"

Pa finally put his foot down. "That's enough, Rosie. When Ellie was missing, you reminded Jem that God had His hand on her. And on Jem and Nathan too. You know the real guilty are the highwaymen who started it all by going after the gold." He planted a quick kiss on his sister's cheek. "Now, please. No more blaming yourself. Like Mother used to tell us . . ." He paused and waited.

Aunt Rose sighed. "All's well that ends well."

Pa smiled. "That's right. And it *did* end well. The *New World* steamed away with the Midas gold four days ago." He sat down and unfolded the newspaper he'd been carrying under his arm. "And by God's grace, they found more survivors from the *Duchess* than they first believed."

Jem hurried over and found a spot next to Pa. Ellie squeezed in beside Jem. Nathan plopped down on the floor to listen. "Is Henri all right?" he asked.

Pa didn't answer. Instead, he started reading from the front page of the *Sacramento Daily Union*: "Steamboat accidents are of quite frequent occurrence lately. It seems to be an epidemic. Just last month, the *Washoe's* boiler exploded, ushering one hundred or so into an untimely grave.

"Now, another calamity has struck. Last Wednesday, the evening of September fourteenth, the steamboat *River Duchess* ruptured a boiler near the head of Steamboat Slough. A large section of her starboard side blew out, causing much injury and not a few deaths. Great blame rests upon the construction of the boilers, and it is hoped that manufacturers . . ."

While Pa read aloud, Jem silently raced through the tiny print to the names of the casualties. The list of deaths was short—no more than two dozen. Jem sighed in relief when he didn't find Henri or his father listed. Neither were they among the long list of injured.

Jem was pulled back to Pa's voice when he heard, ". . . Captain Belrose is to be praised for his quick action in seeing to the safety of his passengers and crew. While several persons were instantly killed by the explosion, the noble captain's overseeing of the aftermath kept the number of casualties less than it might have been."

Henri was right, Jem told himself. *His father is honorable. He didn't run away with the gold. He stayed with his ship.*

"The survivors and the dead have all been identified," the article continued, "save for that of a colored cabin boy, who is feared drowned. The *River Duchess* is slated for repairs, and the captain expects the ship to be ready for full service by the first of the year."

Pa flipped over two pages, to a tiny square of words. "I thought you might like to see this too." He tapped the article's title: "Union Gold Recovered."

Jem laughed softly while he read how gold from a small dinghy had been recovered along the river near Freeport. Two suspected Knights of the Golden Circle, Clayton Forbes and Marcus Bradford, had been arrested for smuggling, along with two other men. The article didn't mention where they'd gotten the gold, and Jem figured that was best. The *Duchess* wouldn't be smuggling any gold for a long, long time—if ever.

Pa closed the newspaper, folded it, and tossed it aside. Then he put a strong arm around Jem's shoulder and pulled him close. "I didn't say anything when you told us your story the other day, but I've given it a lot of thought. I even telegraphed Mr. Sterling. You helped save that gold shipment, you know."

Jem shrugged. Mostly he was saving Ellie.

"I told Sterling how you traded away your gold to get on board. He wants to repay you some of that."

Jem felt his eyes widen in surprise. *I can buy a new knife! And maybe a little pig from the fair to raise!*

Pa grinned. "So, since you two are feeling better, I see no reason why we can't take in the last day of the fair."

Ellie squealed her joy.

"Thanks, Pa," Jem said.

Pa chuckled. "Don't thank me too soon. I figured you might as well get used to moving around. You'll be bouncing plenty on the stage home tomorrow."

Jem didn't care. That was tomorrow. Today he was going to the fair.

Historical Note

Steaming up and down the Mississippi and Missouri rivers, paddle-wheel steamboats were the lifeline between cities and the frontier during the 1800s. Raw materials flowed into the cities; manufactured goods chugged upriver to small towns and settlements.

Out West, steamers traveled the Sacramento River from the capital of California to the port of San Francisco. Many steamboats had one paddle wheel at the stern (back); others, like the *River Duchess* in this story, had two. These boats were called "side-wheelers," with a paddle wheel on each side controlled by its own steam engine.

The explosion of the *Duchess*'s boiler is based on actual accounts of boiler accidents in the 1800s. Passengers took their lives in their hands when they boarded a fickle steamboat. So many things could go wrong. One steamboat expert compared the risk of traveling aboard a riverboat from St. Louis to Kansas City in 1860 to taking a trip from Kansas City to the moon today.

During the Civil War, steamboat travel became even more dangerous. After two years of piloting on the Mississippi River, Samuel Clemens (Mark Twain) ditched the job. He was tired of being shot at and found new work.

In the West, many Southern supporters rallied around the Confederate Cause. They worked hard to make mischief in California, which had entered the Union as a "free" state by only a narrow margin. Sacramento itself was a hotbed of Southern support.

Each month, three or four steamers sailed from San Francisco loaded with millions of dollars' worth of gold for the Union. General Grant considered California's gold essential for the war effort. But all that gold could just as easily have gone to the South, perhaps changing the course of the war.

Late in the war (1864), real-life Knights of the Golden Circle made a number of attempts to seize California gold and Nevada silver for the cash-starved Confederacy. They robbed stagecoaches and once left a note just like the one Black Boots gave Sheriff Coulter. However, in spite of their efforts, no gold from California ever reached the South.

Visit www.GoldtownAdventures.com to download a free literature guide with enrichment activities for *River of Peril*.

About the Author

Susan K. Marlow is a twenty-year homeschooling veteran and the author of the Circle C Adventures and Circle C Beginnings series. She believes the best part about writing historical adventure is tramping around the actual sites. Although Susan owns a real gold pan, it hasn't seen much action. Panning for gold is a *lot* of hard work. She prefers to combine her love of teaching and her passion for writing by leading writing workshops and speaking at young author events.

You can contact Susan at susankmarlow@kregel.com.